To Many Goodbyes

Maudie Gunier

Order this book online at www.trafford.com
or email orders@trafford.com

Most Trafford titles are also available at major online book retailers.

Printed in the United States of America.

ISBN: 978-1-4269-6329-2 (sc)
ISBN: 978-1-4269-6424-4 (e)

Trafford rev. 11/10/2011

www.trafford.com

North America & international
toll-free: 1 888 232 4444 (USA & Canada)
phone: 250 383 6864 ♦ fax: 812 355 4082

The small girl lay on the lumpy mattress on the old iron bed staring up at the ceiling. The faded walls of the room held a few pictures, and was really the front room, but the large bed on which she lay, was placed in one corner to provide a place to sleep for her older brother. A pot belly stove stood in the middle of the room, the only heat for the four room house with it's thin board walls. It was clean though, her mother, Mae Rosie, saw to that. She scrubbed the old wooden floors down on her hands and knees at least every other week, and swept the floors every day.

The girl got up and walked across the room to look out the screen door. It was so quiet, she wondered where her family had disappeared to while she had fallen asleep in the late morning hours.

"Miss Willer Mae, Miss Willer Mae, your sister done had a big baby boy, and my mammy hep deliver him," Sophy hollered to the eight year old, as Willer Mae came out of the house slamming the screen door with the screen partly torn off. Willer Mae rubbed her large brown eyes with slightly dirty hands, which turned her olive skin tan around her eyes.

"Ha,ha, I got to see him afore you did, and he ain't even my kin. He's white alright, just like you." Sophy jumped around as she told her friend about the new baby. "I was peeking through the winder when my mammy turned him upside down and hit his bottom, and he let out a holler like ah never heard afore."

"Naomer had a baby and ah missed it?" Willer Mae asked, as though it was just sinking into her half awoke mind. "Let's go see it."

The little girls skipped, hopped and ran the quarter mile to the house boat anchored to the Tennessee River bank. The green foliage along the bank waved gently in the mid July afternoon. It had been very hot and sultry, but Mother Nature decided to give the people of Guntersville,

1

Alabama a chance to recouperate from the past days of scorching heat on this summer day in 1932.

The girls walked up the plank leading to the houseboat from the bank. Willer Mae opened the door and stuck her head inside the small room. "Can me and Sophy see the new baby?"

"Why sure child, ya'll come on in," Sophy's mother, Weze said, and led the way to the small bedroom. Willer Mae's mother and two older sisters were gathered around Naomer on the bed as she held her precious new baby.

The baby was uncovered from his homemade flannel quilt where two large dark round eyes darted out from the cover, than closed to go off to sleep, as if bored with the whole room full of women. Straight red hair stood up on his little head consuming all the attention, like a signal from a light house.

"Now, would you young'ns go down to the holler and tell Bo and the other men that he has a new baby boy. They're down there chopp'n wood and building on the neighbor's new home," Mae Rosie told the girls, as she covered the baby back up and fluffed up her exhausted daughter's feather pillow. And Willer Mae, when you get back, you get up yonder to the house and get washed up. My lands! I don't know how ya girls get so much dirt on you," she said.

"If'n your mother knew you took a nap like that," Sophy whispered, "Why she'd wupped you good. That's why I's like being dark, cause my dirt don't hardly show none."

The young girls followed the winding path through the heavily wooded area. They had lived in these woods all their lives and hardly ever paid any attention to the hooting of the owls or other strange noises in the deep woods unless it was to scare one another. A Doe and her young Fawn walked across the path in front of them and turned to look back when she heard the giggling of the girls.

"Oh look, Willer Mae," Sophy said, as she pulled one of Willer Mae's long dark braids to stop her.

"What a cute little Fawn. Come here little baby," Willer Mae slowly walked forward, but the Doe sensed danger and darted away with the spotted fawn at her heels. They continued walking to the clearing in the woods where the five men were cutting down trees and building on a home. They heard the laughter of the men ring out in an echo through the woods.

"Let's hide behind this here tree," Willer Mae said, "and see what they're a doing afore we barge in on them." They squatted down behind the tree, turning their full attention toward the men who were sitting around a large sawed off tree stump, each holding a handful of cards.

"I'll raise you two cents, R.T.," one of the younger men said as he raised the jug of homemade white lightening over his shoulder and took a long swig of it. "Hey, pass that jug over here. You young'ns are drink'n it all," they heard Willer Mae's father, Carl, say.

"Ooh–, they're playing poker and drink'n shine," Sophy volunteered. "Your mammy would be madder'n a ole hornet's nest if'n she knew."

"Well, I won't tell on em and you better not either, Sophy, ya hear?"

"Well, if ya let me play with your jump rope, I's guess I won't tell," replied Sophy.

"Let's go tell them about the baby," Willer Mae said, ignoring the jump rope issue as she started running toward the men. "Bo, Bo, they sent us to tell you Naomer had a baby boy."

A couple of the men grabbed up the cards and one hid the moonshine jug down by his legs before he thought the girls saw it. Bo grinned as he jumped up reaching for the sky. "Wa hoo!" he hollered, "a boy, a boy, hear that daddy? I got me a boy."

The men all shook his hand and patted him on the back with their congratulations as the two little girls watched. "You better go see that new son of yours," Bo's father told him.

Willer Mae and Sophy followed Bo through the woods back to the house boat talking along the way. "What does he look like, Willer Mae?" Bo asked. "Well," Willer Mae slowly said, as if in thought.

"I know one thing for sure," Sophy jumped in volunteering, "he has a head full of bright red hair."

"Ha! Just like mine," said Bo.

"No, much, much brighter red than your'ns, Bo," Willer Mae finally added.

"Pass the cole slaw, please Ma," Willer Mae's brother, R.T. said, as the family sat around the supper table that evening.

"Naomer and Bo sure have a fine baby boy there," Carl said, and shoved a big piece of corn bread into his mouth.

"My lands, we tied him in a tea towel and hung him from the fish weighing scales and he weighed nine pounds seven ounces. I told Weze I ain't never seen a baby around these parts that big before," laugh Mae Rosie.

"Oh, I wish Naomer and the baby could stay with us for awhile, "cried Willer Mae, "So's ah could hep her take care of him."

"Well, darling, ah suspect ya'll be there a plenty, and Francis and Maggie too," answered Mae Rosie. "Bo's ma, Granny Parker. Can't do too much with her arthritis acting up all time."

Francis and Maggie both giggled. "Yeah, ah know Francis and Maggie will be there a lot. Especially with Bo's younger brother living there now," teased R.T.

"Oh, shut up and mind your own business, R.T." Francis said. "At least he's a lot better looking than that homely ole girl in town ya'll like." "Yeah, R.T.," Maggie jumped in.

"Now young'ns, let's cut the fuss'n." Their father scolded, Francis and Maggie has ta hep Naomer with that there baby during the day, so's there ain't no use argu'n about it.

Everyone was quiet for awhile until Willer Mae asked, "What did they name the baby?" Knowing she was probably the only one that didn't already know.

Mae Rosie proudly answered, "Charles Thomas Parker. Now ain't that a name fit to be president of the United States someday!" she exclaimed.

"President! Ha, he'll be lucky if he ever gets out of Guntersville," answered R.T.

"And what's wrong with Guntersville?" asked Maggie, "I like it here and ah hope ah live here all my life."

"You probably will. You'll marry some ole farm boy and have a dozen ornery kids," he said, as he grinned and spooned some turnip greens onto his plate. Maggie kicked him in the leg underneath the table. "Ouch," he hollered, "Ah feel sorry for your future husband and your future kids," he said, as Maggie kicked him again.

This time Ma spoke up, "now children, let's all cut out this fuss'n and try to finish our supper in peace. The family became quiet again. Their Pa's word was law, but when Ma got a hold of them, she met business. Mae Rosie looked at her family. R.T. was almost grown. And Francis and Maggie were in their early teens. Willer Mae, her baby, was the only one that wanted to be held and cuddled anymore. They all had olive complections and dark hair after her mother's Indian heritage.

"Miss Willer Mae," Sophy hollered, as she walked up to the screen door. "My mammy's over yonder at your'ns sister's houseboat help'n with the baby. Do ya want to go see the baby with mc?"

"Well, ah guess so. Francis and Maggie are there too a clean'n house for Naomer." The summer heat beat down on the girls as they walked and skipped along the path to the houseboat. The humidity was high and sweat ran down their faces. "Oh, it's so hot today!" Exclaimed Willer Mae. "Pa said it'll probably rain this afternoon and cool it down some. I'm just a sweat'n June Bugs. And look at them little critter grasshoppers just a jump'n around today."

"They's must be sweat'n June bugs too," answered Sophy, as she wiped the sweat from her forehead with her dress tail.

Willer Mae danced around pulling her dress over her head. "Sophy I's tak'n my dress off and a jump'n in that water in my underpants. Ah can't stand this here heat any more."

"Oh, that's what I's gona do to," Sophy cried as she copied Willer Mae and pulled her dress off throwing it on some bushes. They played at the edge of the water, remembering the warning of their folks not to get in the river without older people around. They were both good swimmers as they had lived by the river all their short eight years of life, and was taught to swim almost before they could walk by their siblings. The girls splashed each other and laid down in the cool water up to their necks. Willer Mae's long braids felt heavy on her back. She brushed the few strands of misplaced hair in front from her forehead. "Oh, this cold water feels so good," she said to Sophy as she ducked Sophy's head under water.

"Hey, don't do that, Missy, because I'll call out Mr. Water Moccasin snake to get ya," she replied. "I wonder if that ole snake is still around here? Nobody's seen him for a long time, but ya never know. He might be a sneaking up on us right now," Sophy teased. An hour must have passed before the girls decided they were cool enough to start back down the hot trail to Naomer's riverboat.

"Oh, Missy Willer Mae get out of the water quick, cause that ole snakes coming up behind ya," Sophy said from where she had just climbed out onto the bank.

"Oh Sophy, quite teasing. That ole snake ain't around here today."

"Miss Willer Mae, I's ain't a kidding. Now get out," Sophy abruptly ordered her, and picked up a long stick. Stepping down into the water Sophy put the stick between Willer Mae and the snake, as Willer Mae looked back and screamed. The snake was just a few feet behind her. "Get out," screemed Sophy, as she shoved the snake back with the stick. Willer Mae quickly scrambled onto the bank followed by Sophy leaving the stick behind with the snake.

"Ooh, that was close," cried Willer Mae. "You saved my life," she told Sophy, as she hugged her close. "Let's get out of here before that ole snake decides to come out of the water." They stayed on the dirt path along the river to see little Charles Thomas.

"Aw wonder why there ain't never nobody around that old Feldstead home?" Willer Mae asked, as she pointed south into the woods where they could just barely see a big old weather beaten house among the thick trees and brush. "Let's walk over to it," Willer Mae excitedly said.

"Oh, aw don't know, Miss Willer mae, my mammy say's it's haunted."

"Passh, my ma says there ain't no such a thing as haunted houses," Willer Mae said, as she started walking toward the weed grown path that led to the old home, with Sophy following behind.

"Well how does she know?" asked Sophy. "It could be and it couldn't be. My folks says Mr. Feldstead poisoned his wife and daughter and than hung hisself, but someone came along and found them and took the wife and daughter to the doctor and they's got okay. But than they's moved away and no ones ever heard from them since.

"It looks like it was a nice home one time, Sophy, was they rich?"

"My folks says they was, but they started having money troubles, as to why the father did that, and wanted to kill em all. In fact, my daddy, when he was real young, used to to do yard work and hoe their garden for them. He said Mr. Feldstead was real strange. The girls stopped in front of the house and stared up at the two story home with some of the window shutters barely hanging on to it. "Ain't it creepy," quivered Sophy.

"You're just a lettin your magination run away with you, Sophy. I bet it's beautiful inside."

"Well, I's leav'n. I's not going into a creepy ole house where some crazy ole man hung hisself," cried Sophy.

"Sophy, come on, please, let's go in and see what it looks like," begged Willer Mae.

"You go ahead. I's a waiting right here for you, but you better not scream for no reason and scare me half to death. After all, aw saved ya from that ole snake today."

"Okay than, I'll just go by myself, but don't expect to play with my jump rope any more," Willer Mae said trying to act mad like she really meant it.

"Aw don't care. I's ain't a goin in there and ya shouldn't neither."

Willer Mae opened the big heavy door and peered inside. Some mice scurried into hiding, but she was used to mice and hardly noticed them as she glanced around the large living room. A musty odor enveloped everything. An old faded rose colored chair sat next to a beautiful rock fireplace which covered an entire wall. The poker and small shovel still lay on it's hearth. Scattered ashes lay about from a fire there years before. The rest of the down stairs was almost bare except for a huge table with a cutting board on top in the kitchen.

Some grey squirrels ran across the room when they heard Willer Mae enter the kitchen, but she paid little attention to them and kept on with her venture of the downstairs to the front door where Sophy was waiting on the path below. "Come on, Sophy, there was nothing downstairs cept some old mice and squirrels, and they ran away. Please go with me upstairs."

"Are ya sure ya didn't see or hear anything scary?" "No nothin," answered Willer Mae. "Alright, but ya have ta play whatever I's want to play for two weeks, okay? And ya have ta let me play with your'ns jump rope." "Okay," Willer Mae agreed.

They climbed the winding stairs slowly holding on to the once beautiful oak banister, afraid of what they may find at the top. "Sophy, isn't this here stairs beautiful? Can ya magine the ball dances they had here years ago. And the garlands of Pine and Holly decoratin this here banister at Christmas?"

"I's too scared to talk," answered Sophy.

At the top was a very wide hall with doors leading into five bedrooms. The old wood floors were almost bare of the carpeting from age, mice and other rodents which had taken the house over. The bedrooms were bare of furniture except for the last one they entered where a small bed was with a faded pink canopy top and matching bedspread. A dresser set beside it, and an old tarnished silver brush and mirror lay on top.

"Oh, the daughter must of had this here room," said Willer Mae.

"Well, I's hope she's still alive, so's that her spirit can't haunt this room," quipped Sophy.

"Oh Sophy, there ain't no spirits here. When you die, ya either go to Heaven or Hell, depend'n on how good ya are," Willer Mae said as she picked up the mirror and held it up to her face. A loud boom frightened the girls as they jumped in terror staring at the ceiling where a door had opened into the attic.

"Now who did that?" whispered Sophy, as she stood scared stiff.

"I's think we just jarred it open walking around in here," whispered Willer Mae back. She slowly walked around the opening looking up into the attic. "It's light up there. There's some winders in the attic aw betcha. It looks pretty light up there. I'm gona get that chair that I's seen in the hall and look up there."

"Not me, I's getting out of here," replied Sophy.

"Sophy, please don't leave me. I'll give ya my doll if'n ya stay." Sophy stayed and Willer Mae climbed on the chair but was still too short to boost herself up enough. She could barely reach the top with her finger tips. "Wait, I think aw feel something," she said, as she pulled a board down which extended into a ladder.

"Willer Mae, are ya sure ya want ta go up there?" "I's have ta see what's up there," she quipped as she started up the old ladder.

"Oh Sophy, she exclaimed, "Ya can't believe what's up here. A little table and chairs with dishes on it and a doll and teddy bear sitting on the chairs."

"You're just a funnin me now, Missy Willer Mae. I's don't believe you one teeny bit," Sophy said with a little anger in her voice. Youse just want me to climb up there and aw ain't a goin too."

"Look Sophy, I'll hold the doll up for you to see. She's beautiful, with a yellow dress and bonnet on. Well, their kind of faded, but she has little white socks and shoes on."

"Oh my goodness!" exclaimed Sophy, when she saw the doll. "I's just don't believe it."

"Now ya want a come on up and see what else is here?" asked Willer Mae.

Sophy's eyes widened when she saw the table neatly set with all the little dishes and cups and the old brown teddy bear sitting in a chair ready to eat. The girls looked around the musty room where an old rocking chair with a broken arm sadly sat from years of abandonment. A few empty baskets were scattered around a large box of Christmas ornaments, and a trunk with a snap on it.

"What could be in that ole trunk?" Willer Mae wondered out loud.

"Maybe nothin, maybe a dead body," answered Sophy, her dark eyes dancing between fear and excitement.

"Look at all those Christmas ornaments, Sophy, ain't they pretty," Willer Mae said, as she held a large round whitish clear bulb up to the window, watching a snowman dance inside.

Sophy picked up a China Angel, "Oh, it's beautiful," she whispered and blew the dust off of it. "Aw ain't never seen the likes of these ornaments before. Why we's just string popcorn and cranberries, if we have em, on our Christmas tree and make paper figures, if we have any paper."

What do ya suppose is in that there trunk?" Willer Mae asked again.

"Are you a gona open it?" Sophy asked.

"Of course we're a gona open it, silly," she answered, as she walked over to it and tried to unsnap the snap that was on it. The snap wouldn't budge. "It's rusty!" Willer Mae exclaimed. "It won't open, oh darn."

"Omm–, you shouldn't swear. It might be the good Lord above that won't let ya open it. Like I's say, might'n could be a dead body in that there trunk."

"Oh, Sophy, ya maginations a running away with ya again."

"Listen, did ya hear somepin?" asked Sophy. A door slammed downstairs and noise which sounded like footsteps echoed through the house. "Oh Lordy, Miss Willer Mae, we gona get caught up here. Oh, it sure's hot up here. I's need somepin to drink."

"Shu– be quiet, Sophy, maybe they won't come up stairs."

They heard nothing else. Whatever it was, there was only dead silence now. The girls didn't dare talk above a whisper. They waited what seemed to be a hour to them before they climbed down the ladder, and carefully put the folding latter back up before they sneaked out the front door, the way they came in and ran down the overgrown path.

"Oh, I's glad to get out of there alive," Sophy whispered.

"Who do ya spose that was?" asked Miller Mae.

"Or what did we's hear," asked Sophy, "I's told ya it was haunted."

"And aw told ya there ain't no such thing as a haunted house," answered Willer Mae.

"Well, how do ya knows for sure it ain't haunted. You're just a little girl too, ya don't know everthing." They dropped the subject of the haunted house and walked on toward the houseboat to see little Charles Thomas. The afternoon heat still blazed down on the girls. They stopped once at the rivers edge and cupped water in their hands to drink.

"Aw bet ever ones a wonder'n where we are. Sophy, aw think we's better not tell anyone about goin in the ole house yet. I's think we's should go back there and see what we can find out. See if'n someones a livin there. We's got to see what's in that ole trunk."

"Oh, aw ain't a goin back there, uh, uh, ya ain't a gona git me back in the ole haunted house, no siree. How ya think ya gona get that ole trunk opened anyway?"

"Aw'll think of somethin, don't worry." Willer Mae answered. "Well, I's won't worry, cause I's don't wana see what's in that ole trunk," answered Sophy.

"Sophy, wouldn't ya like to go play with that doll and teddy bear and them little dishes? And maybe we could even keep them if'n they don't belong to anyone any more. Now, don't say a word to no one and let me think for a few days of a plan, okay?"

"Okay, I's promise aw won't tell no one," she hesitated, "for awhile anyway."

"Do ya girls want some cookies and milk?" Naomer asked her little sister and Sophy. " "Dad just brought some fresh cow's milk over, and aw just baked a batch of ginger bread cookies this morning."

"Yeah, we're starved," both girls said together. "Did my mammy leave?" asked Sophy.

"And where's Francis and Maggie?" asked Willer Mae.

Well they all left. It's four o'clock, almost time to get supper," she added.

"Anyway, we came to see Charles Thomas," Willer Mae said, as she bit off the arm of a ginger bread man.

"Yeah, we's hope he's growing, so's he can play with us someday," quipped Sophy.

"Well, that'll be sometime from now, girls, don't ya'll have any other kids around here to play with?" "Not in the summertime when schools out," answered Sophy. "Just me and Missy Willer Mae."

"We been swimming in the river, it's so hot," Willer Mae told her sister. "Ya'll be careful in that river. Ya know there's Water Moccasins in there," warned Naomer.

"How old are ya, Miss Naomer?" asked Sophy.

"Aw just turned seventeen."

"You're so pretty," said Sophy, while leaning on her elbow and looking up at Naomer.

"Why thank ya, Sophy, and aw think you're cute and pretty too."

"Naomer, do ya know anything about the old Feldstead home that everonc says is haunted?" Asked Willer Mae.

"Well no, Aw never believed it to be haunted, but ya never know for sure," she answered.

Willer Mae looked at Sophy who was jittering about, and she knew she was about to blurt everything out if she didn't stop her. Just as Sophy opened her mouth, Willer Mae pulled one of Sophy's short braids hard and started talking herself. "It's a nice old home. I wonder why no one has ever lived there since Mr. Feldstead hung hisself?" asked Willer Mae.

"Probably cause it's haunted," answered Sophy, and was about to say something else when she gave Willer Mae a look to kill, but kept quiet.

"Well, I did hear that an older son of Mr. Feldstead got into some trouble. Something about he embezzled a lot of money from some bank or company," Naomer said, while looking out the window like she was trying to recall what she could about the incident.

"What's embezzled?" Willer Mae asked.

"Well, it's like stealing, but just a slicker way of doing it aw suppose. And than aw recall something about Mrs. Feldstead, who was not the mother of the older son, was going to leave Mr. Feldstead because of this trouble. And it seems like she had a boyfriend in another town. But than ya hear a lot of rumors.

A cry came from the bedroom and Naomer fled and returned with Charles Thomas. His vivid red hair stood on end as he curiously looked at the little girls and started to cry again, but was soon laughing at the funny faces they made at him.

September came with the excitement of school starting throughout the Greene household. Willer Mae and Sophy would both be in the fourth grade at a small country school a mile from their home, where about twenty five children attended from the first grade through the eighth. The older Greene siblings were all in high school, which was about a half mile past the grammar school, so they all walked to school together.

Mae Rosie, Francis and Maggie had been sewing on the new school clothes for several months. The three girls each got two new dresses and R.T. two homemade shirts and two store bought pairs of pants. Carl had sold several young calves to buy the material and also bought each of them a new lunch pail and a few school supplies.

The weather was turning cooler and a fall crispness whispered through the land. Soon the leaves would start falling and talk of an early snow was predicted by the older folks around Guntersville. A squirrel scampered up an old oak tree in front of Willer Mae's house as Sophy came up the path jumping rope.

"Miss Willer Mae, I's got a new jump rope. Do ya want a come out to play?" she hollered through the torn screen door.

"Be right there," Willer Mae answered, as she crawled under the iron bed in the front room to get something she wanted to show Sophy.

"What's that?" asked Sophy as Willer Mae stepped outside.

"It's my pa's hacksaw that aw sneaked. We're gona open that trunk with it," Whispered Willer Mae.

"I's ain't a goin back to that haunted house," answered Sophy.

"Now Sophy, I's know you wanta play with that doll and stuff, and see that China angel again, don't ya?"

"Well yeah, but I's scared. Ain't ya scared?" Sophy asked.

"Yeah, but I's more curious to see what's in that there trunk. And I'm a gona go back right now. Now are ya comin or not?" Willer Mae asked as she started toward the path to the old house. Sophy followed behind a ways.

"Sophy, has ya told anyone about what we found there?"

"Well, I's did talk to my mammy some about it, but she only told me I's magin things again and she don't believe me none." "Good," implied

Willer Mae. "I's didn't think anyone would believe ya, if'n ya did say somethin."

Instead of going up the path to the house they sneaked behind the trees watching very closely for anyone around the yard before they dashed up to the huge porch which encircled the entire home. Then they peeked into the windows around house, but no one seemed to be there.

"Aw just wonder why no one ever moved into this house again?" Willer Mae whispered, with Sophy clinging on to her. "It sure was a big old beautiful home once." They quietly opened the door and walked though the downstair rooms. The smell of wood smoldering lingered throughout the house. "It looks like someone had a fire a goin' in the fireplace," Whispered Willer Mae.

"Oh my lands!" their a gona find us in here and kill us," squealed Sophy. "Sh–, Sophy, be quiet so's we can investigate."

"Look Missy, here's a pot with some beans in it and some tobacer butts laying in this here fireplace," Sophy said, as she peered inside the fireplace.

"Well, now ain't that proving there ain't no ghost or spirits here?" Willer Mae said, proud of herself that she had proved Sophy wrong. "But then aw don't reckon anyones a livin here, cause there just ain't no furniture or dishes here neither," she said as they walked through the empty rooms.

"Do ya spose a bums a livin here?" Sophy asked, "Or maybe ghosts eat and smoke to." "More likely a bum, Sophy," Willer Mae answered. Now come on let's go upstairs and start on that trunk."

"Ya mean ya still want to go upstairs now that we know somebodys a staying here?" Asked Sophy.

"Well that trunk and stuff don't belong to them. And aw thinks we all should find out what's in it, and get down to the bottom of this," answered Willer Mae.

The house was silent as the girls quietly climbed the winding stairs trying not to make them creak. They checked all the rooms before Willer Mae pulled the chair up and climbed on it to pull the ladder down. They slowly climbed up to the attic and found everything just as they had left it three weeks before.

"Now Sophy, ya stay right here by the open'n and listen for any noises while I's saw this here snap into."

"Oh Missy, what if'n there's somep'n terrible inside, like a dead body," Sophy groaned.

"Oh poo, there ain't gona be no dead body in there," She said, while she started to saw on the snap. "I's been practicin sawin at home on logs and steel and stuff so's aw would know how to do this, but this might take a long time.

"Well, don't cut yourself, Missy," Sophy quipped.

Willer Mae worked a good twenty minutes sawing and twisting the snap. Sophy listened intensely for any noises, but the house was still. Not even the squirrels or chipmunks were around today. "I's just about got it cut, Sophy," Willer Mae said with excitement in her voice. "There, got that rusty ole snap off. Now come here, Sophy, so's when aw open the top you can see what's in here too."

"Oh no, Missy, I's don't want to see unless ya say it's safe to look."

"Okay, fraidy cat," Willer Mae said, as she slowly lifted the top back till it stopped on it's own. "Well, looks like just a bunch of little boxes."

Sophy moved closer and peered into the trunk, "Sure smells musty, yak----," she made a funny face.

"Let's open this box first," Willer Mae said as she lifted the top off of a red heart shaped box. "It's full of old letters," she said, not very enthusiastically.

"Here open this one," Sophy said, as she picked up a round tin box with a Victorian design on the top.Willer Mae tugged and pulled on the top until it finally loosened from the rust that was holding it on. "Oh, Sophy, here's a beautiful brouch with a bunch of red stones in it. I's wonder if'n it's real stones or just fake ones."

"I's think the Feldsteads were rich, so's it probably cost lots of money," Sophy blurted out.

"But why would they leave this stuff all in this here attic?" asked Willer Mae.

"Come on open another one," Sophy urged, and picked up another tin box, this one yellow with tiny blue flowers all over it. She handed it to Willer Mae.

"Bet this ole tin hasn't been opened for years." Willer Mae said, as she tried to separate the lid from the bottom. Her fingers turned rusty as she tugged on it. "Wish I's a brought me a knife to use on them."

The lid finally gave and slipped off. "Sophy, look at all the jewelry in here," Willer Mae said as she held up a necklace with a heart pendant. "Look it has a inscription on the back. 'Congratulations Nellie on your 8th grade graduation.' That must have been the little girl's name that lived here–Nellie. The doll and things must have belonged to her," Willer Mae softly said.

"Gosh! They's really do belong to someone," was Sophy's input.

Willer Mae opened the pendant, and a young girl with long blond curls looked out at them. It was inscribed 'From your loving family'. I's wonder what ever happened to Nellie? Is she still alive or where is she?" asked Willer Mae. "Why would she leave this here jewelry." They continued going through the jewelry and holding each piece up to inspect it.

"I's like this pretty gold necklace with the green stone in it best," Sophy said. "I's read a story once about a green Jade stone in a ring. I's wonder if'n that there stone could be Jade?" Willer Mae went on.

"Ya never can tell. This here jewelry might'n be worth millions," quipped Sophy. "What is we gona do about it?"

"Aw don't know. I's got to think about what to do," answered Willer Mae. "But Sophy, doesn't ya dare tell anyone yet till I's decide what to do. Promise?"

"Promise for a few days, but ya better hurry up cause I's don't know how long I's can keep quiet," Sophy told her.

"Wonder what's in this here cigar box?" Willer Mae asked as she opened the lid. "Money," both girls hollered at the same time. "Oh look, hundred dollar bills," said Willer Mae.

"I's ain't never seen a hundred dollar bill before," Sophy told her.

"Well, I's never did neither, Sophy, but I know that little one zero zero means a hundred and not one dollar. One, two, three," Willer mae counted the bills to twenty. "Twenty of them. Let's see, how much money would that be," she encountered.

"Twenty hundred," Sophy quipped.

"No, Sophy, I's don't think you say it that way, but I sure will find out," she said. Willer Mae turned quickly, "Did ya hear that? Sounded like a door slammed."

"Ya, I's heard it."

"Shu–, be quiet, let's listen." They listened, looking at each other with fright in their eyes. "Maybe we's better sneak out of here, but let's open one more box first," suggested Willer Mae, her voice shaking. She picked up a blue paper box with a gold letter F on the front. "Must be for Feldstead," she muttered, as she took the lid off. "Full of paper stuff," she

19

said as she picked up the first one and read, "Birth Certificate of Nellie Feldstead born August 6, 1906. Another one of Elizabeth Squire born February 12, 1874. She must have been Nellie's mother." stated Willer Mae, "This is all birth records and baptism records. Look at all this. Whatever it is, it looks mighty important," she insisted.

"Yeah, sure does," muttered Sophy. "Now let's sneak out of here afore we's get caught".

They quickly put the boxes back in the trunk and closed the lid tightly shut. Then climbed down the latter onto the chair, and Willer Mae lifted the folding latter back into place in the ceiling to hide their secret discovery. Lighting flashed outside of the partially darkened house, then thunder rolled loudly like a whip surrounding them. "Ut oh, we's gona get caught in a thunder storm and I's scared of light'n and thunder," whimpered Sophy.

"It's a start'n to pour, Sophy, we's better wait here awhile till it lets up."

Just then the door opened and a strange man with a beard dripping with water stared at them. "What ya kids doing in my house?" he asked, and lunged toward them grabbing at Willer Mae. "Run Sophy, to my house and get Pa."

"There ain't no need to git your Pa. You young'ns are a trespassin on my property."

Sophy had ran out the opened door as fast as her legs could carry her to get help, Leaving Willer Mae to struggle in her effort to free herself from the scrupulous old man. "Now you listen to me, girl," he told her, while he took a firmer grip on her. Ya kids stay away from here. Do ya hear? Aw don't want ya a sneaking around here anymore or aw'll cut off ya ears," he said and twisted one of Willer Mae's ears. "Now go catch up with ya friend and don't ya tell anyone aw live here or aw'll come a lookin fer ya," he said and pushed her out the open door.

"Sophy, Sophy, wait for me," Willer Mae hollered.

"How did ya get away from that ole man? "Sophy asked when Willer Mae caught up with her.

"He let me go, but he said he'd cut our ears off if'n we come back around or tell anyone he lives there."

"Oh, what are we a gona do about telling?" Ask Sophy breathlessly, as they continued a fast walk through the wooded path toward home.

"Well, aw want ta think about it for awhile, but than aw reckon we better tell my Pa and let him handle it afore that ole bum finds our attic."

The girls excitedly told Willer Mae's parents about what they had found in the attic, and about the old man that was making the Feldstead home his own.

"Well girls, ya'll had no right going in someone else's home, but then I wonder why them Feldsteads never came back to claim their home or belongins. Aw reckon we better notify the sheriffs about the money and things in that attic and let them handle it. Aw'll go to town first thing in the morning. This here storm should let up by then, and expain to um what happened," Carl told the girls and Mae Rosie.

The next evening when Willer Mae's Pa returned home from town, he said the Sheriffs would be at the Feldstead home in the morning to gather up their belongings and board the house up. They told him they would try to contact someone in the family to return the items to, but if they didn't find any of the Feldsteads that Willer Mae and Sophy may be able to claim anything except the home.

"Gosh Pa," exclaimed Willer Mae, "We'ns could become rich with all that there fine jewerly, and how much is twenty one hundred dollar bills, Pa?"

"Well, that's uh—let's see now—that's two thousand dollars, girls," he finally said.

"How long will it take em to find the Feldsteads, Pa?" she asked.

"Oh, aw magin they take a about sixty days. Several months or so," Pa answered.

"Aw, that's a long time," fretted Willer Mae.

"Well child, that'll go by faster than you can shake a finger at. About Christmas time," answered Mae Rosie.

"Am a gona tell Sophy real early tomorrow. Aw magin she's fussin like a June bug," Willer Mae said. "Guess aw'll git to bed early."

"The time slowly went by for Willer Mae and Sophy as they hopefully waited for their fortune. They discussed it at length sometimes, while they imagined all sorts of things happening to the Feldsteads, as to why they never returned to their home or to get their belongings.

Little Charles Thomas was growing and starting to talk baby talk and playgames with them before Christmas that year. The girls taught him to play patty cake and thought he was so smart when he learned his first word "Momma" at five months.

On Christmas Eve a light snow fell, covering the hills and hollers. Everyone in the country side attended church services on Christmas Eve, driving their horses and buggies through the snow with the people wrapped in warm blankets in the open wagons or buggies. The children put on a play about the birth of Jesus and read poems and sang during the service. Each child received a bag with an orange, apple, peanuts and two pieces of hard candy in it along with a gift from the church. The women brought cakes and cookies to serve along with coffee and hot apple cider after the service.

After Christmas was over the people around Guntersville settled into a long winter. Snow still lightly covered the ground and people stayed home by the wood stoves or fireplaces to stay warm. The children were out of school for a two week vacation during Christmas and the snow was almost gone before school started again.

"Pa, when do ya think the Sheriffs will tell us if they found some of the Feldsteads?" Willer Mae asked one day. "Sure thought they would of found somethin by now," answered Pa. "When aw go into town again, I'll stop by the Sheriff's office and talk to em."

"Ma said sixty days would be around Christmas time and it's already way passed," she said.

"Well, sometimes it takes a long time for these things to get settled, baby. Try not to fret and be patient. Shouldn't be too much longer," Pa said gently.

"June Bugs!" Willer Mae sounded bored. "Aw wish I's could walk to Naomer's and see little Charles Thomas. He must really be growing and aw haven't got to see him hardly none this winter." No one answered Willer Mae. They were all busy concentrating on what they were doing. Ma was embroidering on a tea towel; Pa was playing softly on his harmonica; Maggie and Frances was looking at the new spring Sears catalogue in the bedroom; and R.T. was whittling on a piece of wood with his new Christmas knife, carving out a dog.

Only Willer Mae had nothing to do. "Lord, aw might as well not even be around here. No one will talk to me," she said out loud again. And still everyone was so engrossed in what they were doing and didn't answer her.

March came, and Mae Rosie was midwife for Sophy's Ma when she had twin boys on the 5th of the month. Wesey was forty two and this had been a hard pregnancy for her. She had such hard labor that Mae Rosie sent one of Wesey's older sons for the doctor, but the twins arrived before the doctor could get there. The delivery did turn out just fine and the twins were strong and healthy "Willer Mae, do ya want ta walk with me to Sophy's to see how Wesey and the twins are a doing?" Mae Rosie asked. "Sure do, Ma," Willer Mae answered.

The spring air was crisp and cool as they walked along the dirt road. Purple wild flowers were just beginning to peek out of the ground. And the birds were calling to each other repeatedly, acknowledged the hint that spring had finally arrived. Willer Mae and her Ma enjoyed the warm sun on them after the long cold winter.

"Oh come in, Mae Rosie and Willer Mae," Wesey said when she opened the door, the Lord must have sent ya."

"We came ta see how ya'll and the new twins were a doing," Mae Rosie told her. "Well, I's sure glad ya'll came by, cause I's don't know whats to do," Wesey said, as she shooed the cat off the couch so they could sit down. The babies are just a fussin' so and cried all night long. None of us got any sleep. I's finally got them to sleep just afore ya'll got here. They's was just wore out from all their fussin."

"Well Wesey, was they a doubling their knees into their stomachs like it was colic, or how was they a acting?" Mae Rosie asked.

"No Mame," answered Wesey, "It didn't seem like colic at all." Willer Mae and Sophy were quietly looking at new babies which were in pulled out dresser drawers that were placed on top of a small table against the wall.

"Pull up your blouse, Wesey, and let me look at your breast," Mae Rosie said with no embarrassment at all. Wesey did what she was told to do, and they both examined her breast and checked the milk while the little girls knew to keep their eyes on the babies. "Aw think that's what it is, Wesey, ya just don't have enough milk for the two babies."

"What will aw do?" Wesey asked, with a worried note in her voice. "Our old cow is dried up right now." "Well, now don't ya worry none, Wesey, we have a couple of fresh cows and a goat too, but," Mae Rosie said slowly, "a woman's milk would be a lot better. Do ya have anyone close by, Weasy, that could help nurse the babies with ya?" "No, aw recon aw don't know anyone around these parts that is a nursing right now."

Mae Rosie thought for a short while. "Willer Mae, you and Sophy run back to our house and tell Pa ta hookup the horses and go fetch Naomer down here to feed these babies."

"Yes, Momma," proud that she could do something to help out. "Come on, Sophy." and out the house they went hurrying towards home.

"Now Wesey, ya lay down and get some sleep, while them babies are a sleeping. I'll do the dishes and watch the little ones sleep. Where's the rest of your family anyway?" she asked.

"Henry had a job to do for Mr. Wilson," answered wesey, "And ah got the three year old to take a nap in the other room. The older kids are down the road at some friend's house."

"Ya go lay down now, ya hear?" Mae Rosie told her.

"I's hate ta leave ya sitting here all alone, but I's is awful sleepy. Didn't get hardly any last night."

"Ya go right ahead. Don't worry none about me," she said and pushed her gently toward the bedroom. Mae Rosie sat there until she heard Wesey lightly snoring, which didn't take long for her to fall asleep as exhausted as she was.

She looked around to see what she could start on first. There was a pile of dishes in the sink and on the counter top, and the bare wooden floor needed sweeping badly. Deciding to sweep first she looked around for a broom and found it on the back opened porch by the steps. She glanced around the back yard. Two hound dogs lay beside their dog house under the shade of a tall oak tree. The chicken house was some distance beyond the dogs, and three pens holding fighting cocks were close to the chicken house. She stopped to think how glad she was that Carl had gotten rid of his fighting cocks. It was such a cruel sport with no meaningful purpose at all just the wasteful gambling and pain and death to the chickens. She wondered why men liked fighting, war or any kind of fighting.

Wesey had a hard life, Mae Rosie thought. She knew she was forty two, almost to old to have these twins. Henry was a good man, except when he got to drinking moon shine. A few times she heard he had hit Wesey and the children. She guessed he had settled down some now

25

that he was older, and their two older children were both married. The four younger children were still home plus the twins now. She had known Wesey for about ten years, since her and Carl had moved to their home down the road where they share cropped. Most of the white folks around had nothing to do with the colored folks, but her family's views were different. They believed everyone was equal, no matter what race or color.

The floor looked better now that it was swept, and she started on the dirty dishes. She knew that Wesey kept a clean house, but with the new babies it was hard on her. Another hour went by before Mae Rosie heard the horses and wagon coming down the road. She pulled back the dusty curtain and could see Carl helping Naomer out of the wagon with little Charles Thomas. Willer Mae and Sophy jumped down from the wagon and ran to the old swing hanging from an oak tree.

"Wesey and the babies are still a sleeping, but they's should be a waken up any minute, dear," Mae Rosie told Naomer. I hope you don't mind, ya were the only nursing Momma around here right now that we all could think of."

"Oh Momma, ya know anytime aw can help out I's proud to do so. And Charles Thomas eats so much now he hardly ever wants to nurse anyways." She said, while she twisted some strands of her long dark brown hair. "Aw can't wait to see them twins. My goodness, twins around these parts are really somethin." She turned toward Pa, "Pa did ja find out anything on the Feldsteads yet?" Her slender body and gracefullness was beyond the beauty of most women in the south lands. Naomer was really not aware of just how lovely she was. Parents didn't talk about the beauty of their offspring. They just excepted the children as they were.

"No, aw hafta go to the Sheriff's office again aw spose and see what's a taken them so long. Willer Mae keeps after me about going. Aw just been so busy plowing and planting the land that aw ain't had no time."

The twins started fussing, and Wesey and her three year old were waking up. Mae Rosie handed one of the twins to Noamer, as she started to unbutton the front of her blouse, and Carl and the children disappeared out into the sunny yard. The hungry baby suckled her breast, making grunting sounds as though it was enjoying the nourishment of the fulfilling liquid. Wesey took the other baby from Mae Rosie and nursed it.

"I's sure do appreciate ya'll and what your family does for me," Wesey told them, as she kissed her baby on the forehead.

"Well, ya'll done plenty for us too, Dear," Mae Rosie answered.

"It feels so good to hold a newborn again," Naomer said, as she cuddled the baby close. "They are just beautiful. They look like they might be identical."

"Now we need to work out a plan," Mae Rosie said with authority in her voice. "Aw think if Carl brings Naomer over once a day and she nurses both babies, along with your breast milk, and a little fresh cow's milk later on, in maybe a week or two that should take care of the twins. We'll bring our cow over here for you to keep awhile."

"Oh, praise the Lord. Everything's gona be alright. Yo sure are good white folks," Wesey said with tears in her eyes.

"Now don't ya fret none," Mae Rosie said to Wesey while putting her arm around her. "These here twins are gona be just fine and grow up to be big and healthy. They sure are enjoying that nursin, but it looks like they's just about ta go ta sleep again."

"Seems only yesterday that Charles Thomas was this little," Naomer smiled.

"Ma, Willer Mae," Pa hollered as he hurried through the front screen door. "Aw talked to the Sheriffs, and the Feldstead's daughter is a comin here ta see Willer Mae and Sophy soon."

"Really Pa, they found her?" asked Willer Mae as she sit up in bed. She had an upset stomach that morning and Ma let her stay home from school.

"But, June bugs, that means me and Sophy won't get a thing of the Feldsteads, Don't it Pa?" Ma interrupted, "Well, the Lord let's happen what happens. It towarrent meant for you and Sophy to have all that money for some reason only known to the Lord."

"But why is the Feldstead's daughter comin here, Pa?" asked Willer Mae.

"The Sheriffs didn't say, but she's staying at Mrs.Young's boarding house now trying to straighten things out," Pa answered, while he wiped the sweat from his forehead with a handkerchief which he pulled out from the back pocket of his overhauls. "Could be she wants to give ya somethin," he continued.

"Somethin good'll come out of this," Ma added "Ya'll just wait and see."

Just then, R.T., Frances and Maggie walked home from school and joined the family in their conversation about the Feldstead's daughter coming to their home. "Aw, we were a hope'n we could keep all that there jewerly and money and stuff," R.T. said with disappointment showing in his voice.

"Weren't yours to keep," said Willer Mae, sitting up in bed with her big dark brown eyes shining. "Sophy and I's found it. And Sophy would of never had the nerve to go up in that attic if'n it weren't for me begging her."

"Well, lotty daw, look who the big hero is. Big pirate Willer Mae," mocked R.T. back at her. "Now children, that's enough fussin," Mae Rosie encountered. "We share in this family, Willer Mae,"

Francis cut in sarcastically, pushing her long dark hair away from her face. "Well, we ain't getting nothin anyways," concluded Maggie in her slow southern draw, "So why ya all a fussin."

"That's right," Ma said, "and the good Lord will see ta it ya don't get nothin if ya'll keep this here fighten up."

"Am sorry," R.T. said, "Aw know we're family and we'ns shouldn't fight. Aw love ya all a whole lot. More'n ya' ll know."

"Now, that's how aw like to hear my kids talk," answered Pa, "Now ya all didn't let me finish my story. Nellie Feldstead is a coming here to the house Saturday ta thank the girls and maybe ta explain as ta why they left all them belongings here."

"Ya girls will have ta hep me bake some pies and clean the house spotless," Ma told them.

"Oh, Ma, your house is always spotless," R.T. said. "Well, it could be a lot more so aw recken. Aw been a helpin Wesey so much lately, aw kind of let my work go. Ma looked around. The bare wooden floors would need sweeping and mopping with lye. And the checkered table cloth would have to be washed and starched and ironed. She would put a fresh bouquet of flowers on the table too, and use her good saucers to serve the pie on. The strawberries were just starting to ripen, and she supposed she could pick enough of them to make a couple of pies to serve and maybe a third one for Wesey's family while she was baking and the oven hot.

Saturday morning finally came with great anticipation for the whole family. The old house was as spotless as could be with it's unpainted walls where a few family pictures hung, and the table neatly set with the yellow checkered table cloth and a jar of fresh daffodils in the center. Everything was ready for Nellie when she would arrive at ten o'clock this morning.

Willer Mae sat outside in the swing that Pa had made for the older kids when they first moved there. Only Willer Mae and Sophy swung in it now. The swing had been moved along with them from their two former homes, and Pa always hung it from the largest tree in their front yard. Willer Mae looked up at the blue sky as she pumped her legs back and forth, slowly at first then faster as she rose higher and higher. She felt like she was going up into the fluffy white clouds with not a care in the world. No one existed but her....and she would swing forever.

Sophy rode up bareback on her brother's horse and Willer Mae slowed the swing down, back to earth. "Oh, I's glad Miss Nellie ain't here yet," she said, as she slid off the old mare and tied her to a tree. "I's wonder if'n she'll be comin in a horse and buggy or in a car?"

"Why I's magin in a car, silly. She's probably still very rich ya know," answered Willer Mae. "I's just can't magin why she wants ta meet us."

"Do ya think she might give us somepin?" Sophy asked hopefully.

"Don't know, Sophy. But we did find her things. Even if she don't, I's still glad we found her stuff and she got em back. Ya want to swing, Sophy?"

"I's guess so, if'n ya don't swing me too high."

Willer Mae jumped out of the swing and Sophy into it. She was careful not to swing Sophy too high beause she didn't want her to get mad or scared since Nellie Feldstead should be coming any minute. She was also careful not to get her good blue dress dirty that Ma had insisted she put on for Nellie's visit. Sophy was also in a pretty yellow dress and had white shoes on she usually only wore to church.

"Listen," Sophy said, as she quit pumping her legs in the swing. "Aw hear a car a comin."

Willer Mae stopped pushing her and listened too. "Must be Miss Nellie," she offered. "Sounds like a big car." she ran to the front screen door. "Pa, Ma, everybody, she's comin." The car rounded the curve about a quarter mile from their house, while the whole family gathered in the front yard to watch.

A pretty young woman in her middle twenties climbed out of the back seat of the shiny black dodge touring car. The family all stood there in amazement as Nellie Feldstead asked, "Does Willer Mae Green live here?" She continued smiling and pushed her long blond hair back from her face as the family still stood there speechless.

Mae Rosie stepped forward, "Why yes, Darlin, this here is Willer Mae and her friend, Sophy. Am Willer Mae's mother, Mae Rosie," she said and extended her hand in greeting. "And this here's my husband Carl, and the other children, R.T., Francis and Maggie. Now you must be Nellie."

"Yes Mame, I'm pleased to make your acquaintance," Nellie said. "And I really appreciate you girls finding my belongings," she continued in her well educated southern accent.

"Well just come on in our house, Nellie," Mae Rosie went on while she gestured her toward the front door, "come in out of the hot sun. we'll have some cool lemonade. Oh R.T., tell her driver to get out too and come in out of the hot sun."

The house wasn't much cooler than it was outside. Nellie's eyes circled their humble small living room and kitchen. They sensed that she was use to so much more than their meager existence, but she didn't let on as to what feelings she had about their home. She only smiled slightly and commented on the beautiful daffodils on the table, and how their yellow color matched the table cloth.

One could tell by her clothes that she was still well to do. She wore a two piece pink summer suit and white high heel shoes with a large matching leather handbag. Her driver came in also, and he and Carl sit in chairs in the living room where they could still hear the conversation of the others around the kitchen table.

"Willer Mae and Sophy, I'm just so glad you girls found my mother's journal and records, and the Jewelry and money and everything. I want to give you girls four hundred dollars reward money. I have it right here," she said, as she dug into her purse and pulled out the money, "I'll give it to your mother, so she can hold it for you girls for now," Willer Mae and Sophy watch her with wide eyes and opened mouths. "And I want you both to have the dolls and teddy bear and table and chairs, and dishes and other toys that was in the attic. We have them out in the car and I'll give them to you before I leave."

"Oh thank you, Miss Nellie," the girls both said.

"Now I want you all to know, and all the people in the area too, what I found in my mother's journal, because I reckon there was a lot of talk after we left in such a hurry. My father never killed himself like the newspapers said he did, and my mother couldn't tell them what really happened because our lives were in danger. You probably heard my older half brother embezzled some money from the bank in town he was working for," Nellie continued, "and he did, and served three years in prison for that. But anyway, he ran off to New Orleans where my father had another lumber mill besides the one here in Guntersville before he was caught up with. Now mind ya, I was only ten years old when this happened and I didn't know much of what was going on, but after reading my mother's journal, I understand why we had to flee like we did After my brother did that, nobody would buy from our lumber mill here, everyone boycotted it, and it was going broke, so my folks decided to sell everything and move back to New Orleans. They put the house up for sale and had an auctioneer auction all our furniture except just what we needed until the house sold, and my folks said I could take along my toys." Nellie took a drink of lemonade before continuing. Her eyes became teary, and Mae Rosie patted her hand with affection, while the others starred at her amazed with the story and waiting for what happened next.

"Well, that night after the auction was over and everyone had gone, a big black man came to our house on horseback and told my father that there was rumor that someone had seen my brother during the auction and the Ku Klux Klan was coming that night to get him. Maybe an hour later my father ran in and told my mother and me to get up in the attic and hide because some men on horses were coming. Sure enough there were eight of them in white hooded robes. They searched all through our house for my brother. My mother opened the attic door just enough so we could hear them at times. They couldn't find my brother because he wasn't there, and they got so worked up that they beat my father and then hung him in the living room from the chandelier, but made it look like he did it himself."

"I wanted to try and stop them, but my mother held me back and closed the attic so they couldn't hear me scream. We stayed in the attic all night and cried, too scared that they may be waiting for us to come back, as my father told them we had went home with friends that night. And then too, we couldn't bare too see my father hanging from a rope. After we thought they left we kept checking for the smell of smoke, as we were afraid they would burn the house down, but I suppose they thought it would look more like suicide if they didn't. We were so tired from the auction the day before and from crying all night, but we had to get up before dawn and leave."

"It was horrible seeing my father just hanging there from a rope in the moonlight, but we said a prayer or him and packed a suitcase and left everything else. We hitched a horse to the buggy and went to the Sheriff's office where my mother told him that my father had hung himself and left instructions as to where to send his body in New Orleans. Then we went to the livery stable and sold the horse and buggy, almost giving them away according to my mother, and got on a train for New Orleans."

"Why you poor child," Mae Rosie said and put her arms around Nellie, "My, what you went through."

Nellie dried her eyes with a pretty linen handkerchief she had pulled out of her handbag. "I blocked everything out until I read that journal. I remember my mother always saying we had to go back for our belongings someday, but she died of pneumonia when I was only twelve years old. She tried to tell me something. I suppose it was about our home here and things, but she was so weak she kept going into unconsciousness."

Nellie was quiet for several minutes, "I've been at Mrs. Young's boarding house for several days reading my mother's journal and doing an interview for a story to be printed in the Guntersvill newspaper. There's someone that wants to buy the house too, so I'll be a taking care of that this afternoon and leaving in the morning to go back to New Orleans." "The story will be coming out in the town newspaper in a few days, so I wanted you'll to hear it first. It will also tell that two young girls found my belongings, but their names won't be mentioned."

The girls were all drying their eyes and the rest of the family were somber, before R.T. broke the silence. "What will happen to the men, the Ku Klux Klan that did this, Nellie, will they be arrested now?"

"No Nellie answered, that was seventeen years ago. Probably most of them are dead now, and there's no way to prove who they were, the Sheriffs said. It's best to leave it lie."

Willer Mae and Sophy were more excited over the toys that Nellie left them then they were the two hundred dollars in money that each got. "Ma, I's want ya to take the money and get some new furniture and things for the house," Willer Mae told her mother. "And that big rocking horse, aw want little Charles Thomas to have it. Da ya spose Pa would tote it to him in the horse and buggy?"

"Well, aw reckon so," Ma answered, "We have ta take them some fresh eggs and milk in a few days anyhow, so's we could take it then,"

The family told Naomer the exciting news of Nellie's visit and about the Ku Klux Klan hanging her father. Charles Thomas was delighted with the rocking horse. Willer Mae got on it first to show him how to rock it and he soon caught on, making it rock so hard, they had to slow him down before he fell off. "It's a good thing the horse is too high for him to get on by himself, so aw can keep him from rocking too fast." Naomer said, as she stood up and smoothed the skirt of her faded sundress, and went to the cupboard to get some glasses out for lemonade.

"Think aw'll go chop some of that there wood aw saw laying out in the yard," Carl said, getting up and going outside.

"Aw'll go with ya Pa!" exclaimed Willer Mae. "Oh, can aw take Charles Thomas out too, please?"

"Aw recon, but now ya'll watch for snakes. They're bad around this here river ya know," said Naomer. "Ya'll can have some lemonade when ya come in. Ma, I'm glad they'll went out, cause aw need to talk to ya about Bo.

"Why child, what's wrong?" asked Mae Rosie, as she moved closer to Naomer and massaged her shoulders.

"Bo's been a running around with a couple of his friends drink'n. He come home the night before last drunker than a skunk, and when aw got mad at him and didn't want him ta touch me, he hit me and kicked me in the leg," Naomer said and pulled her dress up to show Ma the big bruise on her upper leg. "and aw heard they was all out with a woman too. The three of them and one older woman, Ma. Ya know what she must be." Naomer put her head into her hands.

"Well darlin, aw know that's not right, but sometimes men just have to grow up first before they's become good husbands. Just be patient and if it keeps up, tell me and aw'll have ya pa to talk with Bo. The men here in the south all run around some and drink. Am not saying it's right, but that's just how it is. Aw told ya that before ya got married."

"Aw know, but aw thought it would be different for us. Bo just ain't the same as he use to be. He use to be nice and more thoughtful, but now he gets so angry and mean over nothin. Just some little thing sets him off. And he hits me a lot now and threatens to hit Charles Thomas, and aw ain't a gona put up with it, Ma," Naomer tearfully said.

"Aw know men ain't always what they seem to be, darlin. Where is Bo today?" He's down working on buildin the neighbor's new home. Tomorrow he plans on going fishing for a big catch to sell to the grocery markets. We're broke and need some money to git by on. His pa and brothers will be a going out with him. Aw sure do appreciate the milk and eggs ya'll brought cause aw didn't know what we was goin to eat for a few days. Aw got some tamaters and onions growing, but that's about it."

"Well, Lordy, Naomer, we'll bring ya some of that pig we just butchered. Maybe we can trade ya for some fish if they git a big catch."

They were both quiet for awhile gathering their thoughts. "Ma, aw ain't gona have no more kids with Bo, cause aw don't know if am a gona stay with him."

"Lord a mercy, Naomer, how ya gona keep from having kids?" Ma asked. "Aw'll just pray that the good Lord above won't let me have anymore kids with Bo." Mae Rosie wished she knew the answer for her daughter's problems and also could protect her from any heartache. Her and Carl had not wanted Naomer to marry Bo in the first place but now with a child it was almost forbidden to get divorced. Women just didn't leave their husbands, no matter how mean they were. Society looked down on a divorced woman and they were shunned by the community.

"Ma, Naomer, come quick, there's a snake out here," hollered Willer Mae.

"Well ya git up here on the boat and give me that baby, ya hear?" hollered Naomer back, as her and Ma both hurried out on the boat deck. "What kind is it, Pa?" asked Naomer, with fear in her voice.

"Aw reckon he's a Water Moccasin. He went in this here wood pile and aw needs to git him out afore he bites somebody," Pa answered and started unstacking the the wood and putting it in a new pile.

"There he is Pa. Aw see him, right there," pointed Willer Mae towards the middle of the half stacked pile of wood.

Carl grabbed the hoe he had leaned against a tree to use on the snake, but the snake struck it with full force as Carl moved the hoe toward it, making Carl loose his balance and almost falling. Naomer ran off the deck and grabbed a long branch laying on the ground, hitting the snake with it as it came toward Carl. He regained his balance and landed the hoe blade right behind the snakes head knocking it out enough to chop it's head off.

"Yay, for Pa and Naomer they killed the snake," Willer Mae sing. Charles Thomas, who was too young to know anything about snakes clapped his small hands together hollering "snake, snake."

"By dab, will ya look at that Devil. Must be five feet long." Carl said, as he held it up by the end of the tail. "Well, this one sure won't bite no one. Come on, Willer Mae, let's go bury this snake."

"We best be heading fer home, Ma," Pa said, when they returned. "We only got about two more hours of day light left. Aw have ta git ta bed and get up at dawn to start the plowing."

"Aw reckon we better," Mae Rosie said, "By little Charles Thomas. Grandma will see ya later." She kissed him and hugged Naomer. "Aw hope Bo behaves hisself, Dear," she said low enough so that Pa and Willer Mae couldn't hear her. "If'n you need me, ya holler." They climbed into the wagon and waved goodby to Naomer and the baby on the boat deck. Pa snapped the reins and the horse started on the twenty minute ride home along the Tennessee River route.

The years had passed quickly and Charles Thomas was almost five years old. He was looking forward to going to school next fall with the older children. Willer Mae was in the seventh grade this year and was blooming into a beautiful young woman. Sophy and her family had moved away to another town last fall and Willer Mae missed her terribly. Ma said it was for the best though, as the other white children didn't play with the Negro children and the Negro children they kept to themselves and played. This had left Willer Mae and Sophy rejected by both groups. Now Willer Mae played with the white children.

Francis and Maggie were in their last years of high school. They both had serious boyfriends and were planning on getting married after they finished high school. R.T. had quit school to help Pa farm the cotton, corn and other crops, and had plans to marry a pretty little girl from town in two weeks.

In 1933 the Tennessee Valley Authority was authorized by congress to undertake conservation and flood control work in the northern part of Alabama and a large dam was being built to tame the fiery Tennessee River. There was a lot of work around Guntersville now and most of the men went to work building on the dam. R.T. had applied and was notified to start work in one week.

The whole town was getting ready for a late spring picnic. This was the second annual one held, and plans were for it to be an annual affair if this one had a good turn out. The town council was to furnish the pig which would be cooked over an open fire, and to serve ice cold lemonade and tea. The people were to bring prepared hot food, salads, and desserts.

Pa hitched the horses up to the wagon to take his family, plus Naomer, Bo, Charles Thomas, and one of Bo's brothers. They also loaded in the apple and sweet potato pies that Mae Rosie and the girls had made and pa's fiddle and Bo's guitar. Everyone was anxious to get to the picnic, which seemed to make the two and half miles to the town park take forever. There was already a baseball game going with the boys and men when they arrived. The women were preparing the food on the tables, while a group of young teenage girls were off in another area, and the children were playing hide and seek in the woods close by. Five men attended the cooking of the pig over an open fire pit.

Carl looked up at the sky, "Ya know we'ns just might get some rain here today. It's kind of dark lookin way over yonder." "Well Lord, aw hope not," answered Mae Rosie, "It would just ruin this here picnic for everybody." The rest of the family agreed before they all went their separate ways.

Willer Mae was at the age that she wanted to play with the children, but yet she was becoming a teenager and boys were becoming more interesting all the time. She missed Sophy a lot. She couldn't talk to her new friends about everything like she could with Sophy, why they even cut their fingers with a pocket knife and let their blood run together to become "Blood Sisters". She guessed she would never see Sophy again and also didn't understand why white people couldn't get along with colored folks. What was so different?

Francis and Maggie had told her a few things about boys and being in love, but yet she felt they were leaving out a lot of things she needed to know. Being twelve was a hard age she thought. No one wanted to tell her exactly how you get babies. And they were all so secretive. Even Ma kept saying, "In time you'll know everything."

The baseball game ended with a score of seven to five. The men over twenty five years old had beat the younger ones. The cooks rang the big dinner bell and people started coming to eat. Thanks for the food was given by the Baptist Church preacher, and people crowded around, some sitting at the tables while others sat on blankets or leaned against a tree to eat.

"How many people da ya thinks here, Grandpa?" asked Charles Thomas. "Oh, aw reckon about three hundred," he answered looking around at the crowd. "And it still looks like it might come a heavy rain over yonder to the north." he said.

"Well, aw sure hope not. Anyways not till tonight after we git home," said Willer Mae. "Aw don't want it ta ruin the picnic and aw sure don't want us to get wet."

The people that brought instruments started getting them out after they finished eating. A small stage was set up for different groups to take turns playing and the square dancers gathered in certain areas close by. Fast hoe down music was started, but mountain blue grass was also played throughout the day into early evening, and people not only square danced to a caller, but also did the two step and waltz.

"Aw want to dance," hollered Charles Thomas over the music. "Well, come on little fellow, aw'll dance with ya," Willer Mae told him as she took his hand and lead him out to the dance area.

"Come on, Ma, let's shake a leg too," Carl laugh and pulled Mae Rosie up to her feet. "Oh, we haven't danced for years, Carl, don't know if aw still can."

The rest of the family were with their friends except for Naomer and Bo who had been sitting with her folks. Naomer knew Bo had been drinking moon shine with a bunch of men out by the horses and wagons and the few cars parked in that area. Bo got to his feet and held out his hand to Naomer, "My Princess, may aw have the honor?" he asked.

"Bo, ya don't really mean it. You're so mean at home, why try to be nice now in front of everyone?"

"Well, Honey," he drew the words out, "aw really want to be nice to ya tonight if ya'll would just let me."

"Ya, tonight, aw wonder why," Naomer mumbled.

"Just you wait till aw git ya home. Oh—are we a gona have fun, baby," he told her. Naomer knew if she didn't get up and dance with him that he would make a scene in front of the whole crowd of people, so she did what he wanted.

The music and dancing continued on for several more hours before a car came sliding into the parking area and two young men jumped out. "Two tornados has been sighted coming towards Guntersville," they told the crowd.

The dark clouds started to roll in closer and lightening was visible off in the distant followed by loud thunder. The music stopped and people started to hurry to gather up their instruments, blankets, dishes and children and head for home before the storm got there.

"Aw think we'll make it home before the storm get's here, don't ya, Pa?" Willer Mae asked, as Pa started the horses in a fast trot for home.

"Oh, aw thinks so," Pa answered while he used the whip to put the horses into a gallop.

"Are we a gonna git wet?" Ask Charles Thomas, "aw hope so, aw like the rain."

The dark clouds were getting closer and a few sprinkles of rain started falling. It started lightening all around them in the sky and the thunder sounded like cannons close by. They were only about a half a mile from home and the horses were whinning and nervously wanting to gallop faster to get home. "Everyone hold on tight. We're gona make a run for home," Pa said, as he let the horses go faster. It started pouring rain and everyone got soaked.

When they reached home, Bo asked, "Carl, can we take the horses on to the houseboat?" Zeke and me better secure the houseboat better in this here storm," Bo said.

"Well, aw reckon. Are ya gona stay there the night?" Carl asked.

"Guess so, we'll put the horses in that big shed by the river," Bo said, "So they'll be out of the storm. Naomer, ya and Charles Thomas stay here the night with your folks. You'll be safer."

"Ya all be careful, hear?" Naomer hollered over the storm. "We will, we'll see ya all tomorrow," answered Bo and Zeke.

The storm continued through most of the night and kept everyone from sleeping well, except for Willer Mae and Charles Thomas, who felt secure in their environment. They were still too young to worry about storms and tornadoes, and very tired from the all day picnic.

Calmness came in the middle of the night, but the humidity was high. Mae Rosie got out of bed unable to sleep and went out on the front porch. Her long dark graying hair glistened in the moon light. She always wore it in a bun, except at night. She knew the temperature was right for tornadoes, and she always felt like they were sitting ducks during this season. There was the small underground cellar in the back yard near the house, but they couldn't stay there for very long. It was only there if a tornado was sighted than they would go into it.

Naomer opened the front door to join her mother on the porch. "Aw heard ya git up, Ma, aw can't sleep neither. Aw hope Bo and Zeke are alright. Aw git so mad at him and want to leave, but still aw don't want anything to happen to him."

"Darlin, ya do need to decide on something. Charles Thomas needs a brother and sister. Aw don't know how ya kept from a gettin pregnant, maybe the good Lord did do it. Maybe you should leave Bo, ya marriage don't seem to git any better.

"Aw know, Charles Thomas begs all the time for a brother, but aw just can't bring another a baby into this world with a husband like Bo. Half the time we don't have hardly anything ta eat."

Naomer leaned against the porch pillar looking down the road. She was slender and tall like Mae Rosie, and had a lot of her mother's features. Mae Rosie was almost all Indian, Cherokee that had lived about the majestic mountains of the Appalacian range there. Naomer and Willer Mae took more after Mae Rosie than the other children, but they all had her dark hair and eyes. Carl was Irish and English, which gave the children their light olive complexions.

"Am worried about the sightings of those tornadoes. Aw wonder if they hit anything," Naomer said, with a worried look on her moonlit face.

"Lord a mercy, am worried too. Sure wish we all had a radio so we would know what's going on," Mae Rosie told her.

Naomer laugh faintly, "Ma, ya gotta have electricity first. Since that there dam come in, hope it won't be long till we have it," She said. "It's nice being home with ya, Ma."

"Aw love havin ya here, Darlin, and little Charles Thomas too, but he does need a brother or sister."

"Am afraid what Bo might do if'n aw leave him. Aw don't have any where to go cept here with you and Pa, and Bo would go crazy am afraid. Hard telling what he might do, why he may even take a shot gun and shoot us all. He's that crazy, Ma."

"Has he threatened you over leaving, Naomer?" Mae Rosie asked,.

"He threatens a lot, Ma, but then he apologizes like a little kid, and aw guess aw kinda feel sorry for him then. But aw don't really love him anymore. He's been to mean to me to ever love him again," explained Naomer, as she paced on the small porch. The moonlight showed her slender figure through the long white summer gown that Francis had loaned her to sleep in. Mae Rosie got up from the old rocking chair and held her daughter close.

"Darlin, aw didn't realize he had threatened you about leaving or that you really disliked Bo that much. We'll work somethin out for ya, aw promise."

"Aw don't like to worry ya and Pa none. That's why aw kept quiet all these years, and didn't say much, plus the fact I was wrong and should have listened to ya'll about not marrying Bo. But than I wouldn't have Charles Thomas.

"Now Darlin, that's what folks are fer, to hep their young'ns out when they need hep." They were both silent for a few moments. "Aw spose we better start a fixin some breakfast, it's a gettin ta be daylight. They'll be a getting up pretty soon, aw reckon," Mae Rosie surmised. "Come on let's go fix some biscuits and gravy and potatoes and ham. We might be poor but we got food to fix. Just butchered another hog last week," she said as she held the screen door open for Naomer, "And the gardens starting to grow good."

Willer May opened one eye and smelled the delightful fragrance of the ham frying in the big black iron skillet and biscuits baking in the old wood cook stove. "Charles Thomas wake up. Hum—smell breakfast a cooking. Are you hungry?" She asked, nudging him a little.

"Me's a fixin to git up," he said, looking around the room blinking his eyes, then snuggling back under the covers. "Will ya'll push me in your swing, Aunt Willer Mae?" he asked, looking back out from under the covers.

"Aw recon, after we eat breakfast," she answered.

Carl had been out to the barn and returned to say the horses had come home by themselves. "They must a been a scared of the storm last night, and headed fer home," he said.

The family was almost through with breakfast when Bo's younger brother came running up the porch and flung open the screen door. "Twas a tornado hit the river boat last night and Bo and Zeke are both dead," he hollered, "my brothers are dead," he said, slumping into a chair and sobbing uncontrollably.

"The family sat stunned at the horrible news. Finally Mae Rosie jumped up, "My God, a tornado. The boys are dead. Praise God that Naomer and Charles Thomas weren't there!" "Oh my God," Naomer cried and hugged her baby to her, "Your daddys been killed." Charles Thomas started crying along with Willer Mae, while everyone tried to console them. "Ma, aw didn't want this to happen to Bo," Naomer cried, "not this."

After the funeral Naomer and her family went through what was left of the riverboat. Almost everything was destroyed. They did manage to find some of their clothing that was still good and a few small toys of Charles Thomas. The beautiful rocking horse that was once Nellie Feldsteads was in hundreds of pieces scattered everywhere.

Naomer and Charles Thomas moved back home with her family. The small four room house was crowed for eight people, but R.T. and his girlfriend, were getting married right away at a small family wedding. Frances and Maggie would be getting married this summer after graduation from high school.

Naomer seemed happier now, and Charles Thomas loved being with his aunts and uncle and grandparents. When Mae Rosie mentioned to Naomer that Charles Thomas didn't seem to miss Bo much, she agreed and said she had noticed too. "Ma, Bo never paid much mind to Charles Thomas. He hardly ever played a thing with him, and he told him to 'hesh up' all the time cause he was a makin too much noise. He even hit him a couple times cause he thought he was too noisy, but aw told Bo don't ya dast to hit him again, or aw'll jump on ya myself."

"What did he say to that, Darling?" Mae Rosie asked.

He said don't get all hep up about it, that Charles Thomas needed more learnin. But I could see that Charles Thomas was a gettin askeered of him."

"Well, let's don't talk about the dead no more, Darlin, let him lay in peace. Rest his soul."

School ended in June and wedding plans were buzzing around the Green household. Frances and Maggie decided to have a double wedding the end of August with the family and very close friends, which made a guest list of about sixty people. Hopefully they could all squeeze into the little church. Naomer and Willer Mae would be their matrons of honor and the groom's brothers would serve as the best men. Charles Thomas would be the ring bearer and a little sister of one of the grooms would be flower girl. R.T. was to serve as usher and see that everyone in the wedding group was in place.

Mae Rosie, with the help of all the girls were making the wedding gowns. Their old treadle sewing machine worked slow, and hours were spent sewing on the long white gowns. They also did the intricate stitching by hand adding layers of lace around the skirts and bodices of the gowns. They kept the heavy cast iron heated on top of the wood cook stove to iron the seams and the material. It was Willer Mae and Charles Thomas' job to poke corn cobs and wood into the stove to keep it hot for the iron.

Willer Mae was also learning how to sew on the machine quite well, and her stitching, Ma said, was very good for her age. They gave Charles Thomas little scrapes of material with a needle and thread and thimble to keep him busy while they worked.

"Aw wish school was a startin so's aw had some kids to play with," he kept repeating ever so often. "Well, ya'll have to wait awhile, son. Next month, right after the wedding, school will be a startin for ya," Naomer humored him, and tossled his bright red hair with her hand.

"Maggie let's try this gown on ya so's aw can see if these here tucks are right at the bodice," Mae Rosie told her, and lifted the gown over

Maggie's head. The gown conformed to her slender figure like a graceful white swan as she whirled around in it. "Oh, it's beautiful," the girls commented.

"Maggie darlin, you and Frances will be the envy of all the young girls there," Mae Rosie told her, "Now come here before you soil it." and she slipped it over her long dark hair that hung in wringlets down her back.

Mae Rosie looked at her four lovely daughters. She was very proud of them. They were all slender and tall, with Maggie being the shortest. Their dark round eyes captured their faces all looking very much alike. They were very kind hearted loving girls also, but yet they had hot tempers if something was unfair, and quite a few arguments had resulted through the years growing up together.

Her eyes wondered to her precious grandson. He did favor her family with his big dark brown eyes, but definately had Bo's red hair and freckles which was becoming more evident as he grew older. Maybe it was a blessing that Naomer had not had any more children with Bo, she thought. How would she take care of them now. There was hardly any work in Guntersville for a man, except on the new dam that had come in, let alone a woman. She scensed that Naomer was getting restless when she mentioned looking for a job as soon as Charles Thomas started school.

The wedding was taking all their small amount of savings, but Mae Rosie wanted the girls to have beautiful memories of their wedding day and perhaps it would help them have a better start in their marriages. Naomer and Bo had only wanted their families at their wedding, and she wore a simple white sundress with pink embroidered flowers on it and a bouquet of pink roses.

If the fall crops were good this year perhaps she and Carl could start saving again. Only Willer Mae, Naomer and Charles Thomas would be living at home with them.

On the day of the wedding, by time they got to the church with the wedding gowns in the wagon they were kind of wrinkled. Mae Rosie and Naomer had wrapped them in sheets and layed them across the girl's laps to keep them clean.

"They'll do just fine now girls," Ma told them, "at best their clean and the wrinkles will come out after ya have them on fer a spell. Naomer and Willer Mae helped the brides slip the gowns on and took the homemade rag curlers out of their hair at the church. They brushed their hair out and let it flow over their shoulders almost to their waist. Willer Mae handed the brides their small bouquets of red and pink roses and fern which the girls had made that morning from the rose bushes and fern in their yard. They all had taken special care of the rose bushes this summer to ensure having plenty of roses for the wedding.

Naomer peeked out of the class room door where they were getting ready and saw that the church was almost full of family and friends. She smoothed the front of Willer Mae's rose colored gown and checked her own of the same color.

R.T. walked past his nephew outside who was talking to a distant cousin he had not seen for awhile. "Charles Thomas come and get lined up we're just about to start," he said as he walked past the boys into the back church door. The little boys were playing with a pet baby squirrel that the cousin was raising.

"You can take him home for awhile and keep him if'n you want to," the cousin said.

"Can aw really?" asked Charles Thomas. "Sure take him right now."

"Charles Thomas come in here right now," R.T. hollered out the back door. Charles Thomas put the baby squirrel into his suit pocket which was quite deep, and the baby squirrel fit in there perfectly.

The music started and Naomer and one of the bridesgrooms went first down the isle followed by Willer Mae and the other bridegroom. The little flower girl next, throwing rose pedals along the isle. Charles

Thomas followed carrying the small pillows holding the rings. He had never worn a suit before and was pulling at his shirt collar and tie. The crowd laugh, knowing how uncomfortable he probably felt in a new outfit and it was starting to get hot in the church.

The wedding march begin. Mae Rosie stood up, turning toward the entrance, while the guests followed her actions as the brides started down the isle with Frances on the arm of her father and Maggie on R.T.'s arm taking them to their perspective grooms. The crowd was in awe at the beauty of the sisters in their flowing gowns. Carl returned to his seat beside Mae Rosie, patting her arm while she dabbed at her eyes with a hanky.

Just about when the wedding vows were all said and the couples were about to say their 'I Do's', the baby squirrel decided to crawl out of Charles Thomas's pocket and see what was going on. Charles Thomas didn't feel it crawl out as he was busy trying to pull and loosen his tie and collar with one hand and hold the ring pillow with the other hand. The squirrel looked around at all the people and decided a safe place was to crawl under Maggie's wedding gown to hide. All of a sudden Maggie started jumping around and screaming and two elderly ladies near the front row hollered out, "My Lord, the Holy Ghost done hit her," and the ladies started jumping around and talking in tongues. The crown watched in amazement not knowing what was going to happened next.

About this time Charles Thomas noticed the baby squirrel wasn't in his pocket and took after it just as it ran from under Maggie's gown down the alter steps and the isle to the front door of the church with Charles Thomas and his little cousin in pursuit.

R.T. went up on the church stage and apologized to the guests, "Aw recon there was a pet squirrel got loose, but the boys caught him, so relax and let's enjoy the rest of the ceremony," he said, as the crowd roared with laughter.

Maggie regained her composure as well as the wedding party, and the crowd became quiet as the minister joked a little before he returned to the vows. A reception and potluck on the church lawn followed the wedding with everyone helping, leaving the family free to enjoy their guests. There was a lot of scheming and talking going on behind the wedding couple's backs about a shivare.

"Aw think we all should kidnap the brides," one fellow said, "What da ya'll think about that?" he asked.

R.T. answered, "Well, aw think ya all might have some mighty mad grooms." "Well that's the point. Git em all het up some," the fellow answered.

"Aw got an idear," another young man said, "Why don't we git some hand cuffs from the sheriffs and hand cuff the brides to the wrong husbands."

"Now ya boys are a getting a little sore about this," R.T. went on, "What happened to corn meal in the beds or hiddin all the sheets and blankets."

Just then another fellow hollered, "Hey! We all got two wheelbarrows over here just a waiting for the grooms to push their brides in, Let's go." The group of young men made the grooms pick up their brides and put them into the wheelbarrows and wheel them up and down the road in front of the church while some of the guests followed along behind banging on pots and pans making as much noise as they could. Someone set off a string of firecrackers startling everyone, and this was a shivaree.

Not only this was happening, but some of Maggie's and Francis's girlfriends slipped over to the newlywed's new homes and put cornmeal in their beds.

Maggie and new husband would be living with his folks for about a year while they built their new home on his family's land. Francis' husband had built them a small home about three miles from her folk's home and about two miles from Maggie's home.

The girlfriends also put sugar in the salt shaker and salt in the sugar bowl at Francis' new home, but couldn't at Maggie's because of them living with his folks, but they did pile as much of the furniture in their bedroom on top of the bed, plus everything from the dresser drawers and closet.

Back at the church the grooms had to keep pushing their brides in the wheelbarrows until they were completely exhausted before the other young men would let them stop. Later that evening one of the men grabbed Francis and gave her a long kiss on the mouth before her new husband took a swing at the fellow knocking him down, and the fellow getting back up and hitting him in the nose causing blood to splatter everywhere. The other men were cheering them on before Carl and some of the older men could get the fight broke up.

"It's ten o'clock and aw recon it's about time for everyone to go home," Carl said, "Thank ya all for comin and be careful going home."

Charles Thomas and Willer Mae slept on the way home. The wagon was far less crowed with Francis and Maggie going to their new homes. "Oh, aw miss those girls already!" exclaimed Mae Rosie. "What will we do with all them kids gone?"

"Ya and Pa are going to be so lonesome with them all married now," Naomer told her.

"Well, we still have Willer Mae and now you and Charles Thomas."

"But wouldn't ya and Pa like to be alone for awhile. Of course with Willer Mae aw mean."

"Why no child, we want as many of ya as we can have."

"Well, Ma, Pa," Naomer slowly said, "Cousin Lillian ask me if aw wanted to go with her and her husband, Bill, to California to live. They been there before, and say there's plenty of work in Oakland and San Francisco where they'll be a going."

"San Francisco! Oh darlin, that's worlds away from here. Ya can't go that far from us," Mae Rosie pleaded.

"Now Ma, aw told her aw would think about it, that's all."

"Aw heard that's a bad city, Naomer, a big one too," Carl said. "A lot of bad things go on there they tell me."

"But Pa, aw could find work there. There's nothing here. Nothing to look forward to, but getting married again, and aw don't want to get married again for a long, long time."

"How would ya go? What would you use for money until ya got a job?" Pa asked her.

"Lillian said we could all go on the train and they would pay my way. And Charles Thomas would be free passage. And she said we could get a house together and both pay the rent."

"Just think about it for a long time, darling, we all would sure miss ya both," Mae Rosie said and turned side ways in the wagon to hold her daughter's hand.

The next month was a tearful one for the whole family, as Naomer had decided to go to California at the end of September. She delayed starting Charles Thomas in school, against his wishes, until they got to Oakland where Lillian and Bill said they would live.

Willer Mae started the eighth grade and Charles Thomas teased her a lot about having a boyfriend. "Ya better shet up, Charles Thomas, before aw wupp ya good," she hollered as she chased him around in the house while he chanted, "Aunt Willer Mae's got a boyfriend, Aunt Willer Mae's got a boyfriend."

When the time came for Naomer and her son to leave, the whole family including their spouses, stood in the front yard waving and crying, as the old car with Lillian and Bill and Bill's friend who would drive them to the train station, pulled away. Naomer wiped her eyes as she and

51

Charles Thomas waved back at them from the small back window of the car. Willer Mae stood out on the road waving until they rounded the curve out of sight.

They all enjoyed the train trip, but it was very tiresome. They rolled into small towns and large cities along the way, and watched deserts and mountains appear and disappear through the windows of the train. The beautiful fall colors of reds, yellows and oranges covered the landscaped adding to the excitement of their new adventure.

San Francisco and Oakland were more than Naomer ever imagined them to be. Charles Thomas's eyes were big with amazement where ever he went. The skyscrapers were unbelievable high and the towns were on rolling hills that gave them a weak stomach when they rode the trolley cars up and down the high hills through town.

They found a two bedroom partly furnished apartment in Oakland and the four of them settled in together. Naomer registered Charles Thomas in school, which was about four blocks from their apartment, and she started looking for work. Since she wasn't trained for anything and had never worked before, she knew it would be hard finding something, but she never anticipated it would take her so long to find a job.

Bill got a construction job on a new skyscraper that was going up, and Lillian found a part time office job which didn't pay much, but she was promised raises after the first three months if she was what they were looking for, and it would work into full time.

Naomer didn't find anything the first two weeks, and applied for a course girl dance job the following week. A dark complexion man with an accent, which Naomer thought must be Italian, although she had never met an Italian before, asked her loudly above the music, "can you dance?"

"Yes Sir," she answered. "Well, aw never danced in a show before, but am sure aw can do it."

"Can you do the Can Can?" he asked roughly.

"Well, uh, yes sir, if aw knew exactly what it was, sir," she answered.

"How old are you?" he gruffly asked, as he eyed her from head to toe. "Am twenty one , sir," she nervously answered. "What's your name? Where you from? You speak different than most people here,"

"Naomer Parker, sir. Aw just come out here from down south, from Alabama, sir."

"Do you have dance halls in Alabama, Naomer?"

"Probably in the big cities, sir, aw don't rightly know."

"Sally, he hollered to one of the women walking around in a short dance costume and high heels. Sally walked over looking at Naomer curiously but never said a word. "Show Naomer some can can steps," the man told her. Sally started kicking her legs high in front of her while she stood in one spot.

"Can you do that, Naomer?" he asked.

"Yes, sir." she answered. "Well, come over here by Sally and do it with her," he impatiently told her. Naomer moved next to Sally, thinking she was glad she had wore a full skirt and frilly blouse that day instead of a cotton print straight dress that most of her small wardrobe consisted of. She kicked her legs higher then Sally did and could keep going just as fast as Sally, which impressed the short balding man that had been so gruff.

"Okay, that's good," the man said, and hollered to another man, "Hey Joe, come over here!" Joe hurried over. "I think we found you a replacement for your girl that left. She doesn't know anything about course girl dancing, but I think she can learn pretty fast," he said in his slight foreign accent. "Sally, you can go now," he said and turned to Naomer. "Do the Can Can steps again for Joe, he's the dance coordinator here."

Naomer again kicked her legs high. "Good," Joe said, "We'll give you a try, Honey. After Lou gets your infor he needs, come find me and I'll get you fitted for a custom to practice in."

"Thank you, sir," she answered.

Lillian was home by two o'clock everyday to watch Charles Thomas when he got home from first grade. The day Naomer got the job she excitedly rushed through the door of their apartment right after Lillian got home. "Lillian, Lillian, aw got a job. You'll never believe what doing."

"Why calm down there, honey. No job can be that excitin, can it?"

"Well guess what it is," Naomer rushed her.

"Why hon, aw probably would never guess in a million years. Just tell me."

"Am gonna be a course girl in a fancy nightclub."

"A course girl!" Lillian exclaimed in disbelief. "Now honey, do you'll think ya should be a doing that kind of work? Why what would your momma say?"

"Aw aim not to tell my folks yet, and if something better comes along aw'll quit, but the pay is better than most jobs for women," Naomer said, not as excited now that Lillian didn't quite approve.

"Well, just see how it goes, hon, but be careful in a place like that. Ah hear tell that they can be pretty rough, with fighting and drinking and all that." Lillian hugged her as Charles Thomas burst through the door next in excitement.

"Momma, that ole teacher says aw don't talk right, and she says aw hafta go to a speech thera-simepin, she says."

"A speech therapist. But of course ya talk right, Charles Thomas, Ya just have a southern accent, that's all, just like me and Lillian and Bill. We all have southern accents," she told him and hugged him close.

Well ya have to go see her tomorrow. She sent ya a note," he said as he dug through his lunch pail to find the note.

Naomer sat on a small chair outside the classroom door waiting for the first grade class to be dismissed. She was glad she didn't have to report to her new job until tomorrow or it would have been a problem meeting with Charles Thomas' teacher today. Her nostrils filled with the smell of cafeteria food, sweaty children, paper and glue mixed together in the hall. The bell rang and all the class room doors opened with children rushing out from first through eighth grade.

She entered Charles Thomas' classroom and saw an attractive plump middle aged woman sitting at the desk, and Charles Thomas sitting in his desk waiting for her.

"Mrs. Beckman?" she asked.

"Oh you must be Mrs. Parker," the woman said and motioned Naomer to sit down. "Yes, it's nice to meet ya, Mrs. Beckman."

Now, Mrs. Parker, we have a speech therapist here at our school one day a week." she went on right to the point, "and I feel that little Charles Thomas needs to have some help in his speech."

"Well if ya'll think it will help. Ya know we are from the south, from Alabama, and people just talk like that back there. Plus he does have his two front teeth out and that don't seem to help none," Naomer said, trying to keep her southern accent from being so obvious.

"Well, if it's alright with you just sign this paper for your approval. I certainly feel that it will help him a lot and maybe Charles Thomas can than help you with your speech," Mrs. Beckman told her, and pushed the paper for Naomer to sign in front of her. That really struck a nerve with Naomer, but she signed the paper, said 'nice meetin ya', and motioned for Charles Thomas to come with her.

"He will have an hour class with the speech therapist on Thursdays," Mrs. Beckman said as Naomer walked toward the door.

"Thank ya, Mame," she answered.

"Momma, I don't need to go to no speech therapist," Charles Thomas told her on the walk home.

"Well, son, maybe we all can learn somethin from this here speech therapist. I know they talk so proper here it's just downright discussing."

Charles Thomas laugh at his mother. "What do ya say. Let's give it a try and see. You can teach me and Lillian and Bill to speak properly than.

"Okay, for a little while, but aw don't think aw likes Oakland. It's too big and there ain't even any cows or horses here. And aw can't even have a dog here to play with," he said, looking sadly at his mother with his large brown eyes.

"We won't always be here, Charles Thomas. You can have a dog someday and maybe we'll even live on a farm someday," she assured him.

"Aw hope so. Aw sure miss Aunt Willer Mae and her dogs there, and granny and grandpa and the rest," he went on.

Naomer noticed he was getting to be quite the talker and rattled on about everything lately. Hardly ever was he quiet anymore and she kind of wished he didn't talk so much at times. But she supposed that proved that he was intelligent. They walked quietly for awhile along the sidewalk lined with Elm and Maple trees. The leaves were heavily falling now and brilliant red, yellow and orange colors covered the sidewalks and gutter. They had never seen sidewalks before they came here. Everything was so much cleaner here in the city. The fall crispness hung in the air and Naomer pulled her sweater closer around her chest.

"Won't be too long until the Thanksgiving and the Christmas holidays are here," she said.

"Does it snow here, Momma? Aw hope so."

"No I don't think so. Lillian said she heard it snows here maybe once ever ten years or so, and than just a little bit."

"Shucks! No snow for Christmas. Will Santa Claus find me here, Momma?" he asked with his round eyes big with wonder.

"Oh yes, when Santa Claus comes down from the North Pole he seems to know where everybody lives." "Aw sure hope he can find me. I's have ta write him a letter pretty soon and tell him where aw moved and what aw want."

"What do ya want for Christmas, Charles Thomas?"

"Aw don't know. Maybe a toy car or a toy fire engine, like aw see the big ones go by my school some days. And aw'll just have ta think awhile to see what else aw need. What da ya want, Mamma?"

"Oh, aw don't know either. Maybe a scarf, or a hat and gloves. Aw'll have to think awhile to." Naomer answered, taking hold of Charles Thomas hand to cross the street. She again clutched her sweater closer around her to ward off the cold chill in the air.

"Recon we better send Grandma and Grandpa and Willer Mae something also. Aw sure miss our family this Christmas. This is the first holiday aw ever been away from them."

"Me too. Aw miss them right now," Charles Thomas said almost in tears.

Naomer tried to think of something to divert his attention from this oppressive subject. "Well, aw found a pretty good paying job, so we'll have a very nice Christmas this year, Charles Thomas."

"Momma, aw been a meanin ta tell ya all, can aw change my name to just Charlie? Charles Thomas is jut too long, and the kids at school tease me about being called by two names."

"Well sure, if ya really want to, that's fine. From now on you'll just be Charlie. Aw'll tell Lillian and Bill to just call ya Charlie too," she said and smiled.

The following weekend turned out to be clear and beautiful. It was quite warmer then it had been this fall, and Bill announced he was taking them all to the ocean. "We've been here for over a month now, and aw think it's high time ya'll see the ocean up close!" he exclaimed.

"Ya mean it, Bill, we're a going ta the ocean?" asked Charlie.

"That's what he said, hon. Tell ya what, your Momma and me will fry up that chicken we were gonna have for supper and we'll make us a picnic to take along," Lillian smiled, as she put on her apron and opened the ice box to get the food out.

"A'll mix the potato salad while ya fry up the chicken, Lillian," Naomer told her, while she also tied an apron around her waist.

"Charlie and I," Bill said and cleared his throat, showing that he remembered the proper English that Charlie had taught him, "We'll run down to the little store on the corner and get some of that there root beer and ice to take in a bucket with us"

"Can we get some penny candy too, cousin Bill," Charlie asked as they went out the door.

"Aw ain't, aw mean I never saw anything like this before," Charlie remarked, remembering his English, as he looked out at the vastness of the Pacific Ocean from the rock cliffs where they had parked. "There's a little path going down to the beach. Aw'll tote the picnic basket and we'll walk down there. Looks like a nice clean place," Bill told them.

The waves whipped over the sandy beach and went out again as it had done for over a thousand years before. The four of them pulled their shoes off and got their feet wet when the waves came close. "It smells funny," Charlie remarked, Aw never smelled the ocean before," he held his head high with his nostrils up to take in the scent of the ocean water from millions of species of sea life and sea vegetation that Charlie never knew existed. "Aw like the smell of it."

"Yeah, it's like fresh air mixed with fish and plants. It's a smell that you'll never forget for as long as ya live, aw recon," Bill told him.

The women laid two blankets out and put the fried chicken, potato salad and sliced home made bread out, while Bill opened each one a bottle of Root Beer.

"There's chocolate cake for dessert," Naomer added, "So save some room."

"Boy, ya girls really went all out, didn't ya? Aw won't be able to get back up that path to the car."

Bill took a short nap while Charlie played in the sand at the edge of the water, and the women talked. The sea gulls flew overhead calling to one another, and the sea pounded the rocks in a continuous movement that had no ending.

"Da ya really like your new job, Naomer?" Lillian asked.

"So far it hasn't been so bad. It's kind of fun. Not really like work. Aw still get kind of nervous about it. All that dancin upon the stage in front of an audience, it's somethin aw never thought aw could do."

"Honey, ya a takin to it like a fly to molasses," Lillian told her.

"How's your job a going?" asked Naomer.

"Oh better than ever. They tell me I'm doing good and can have the job for as long as aw want it. I really want to have a baby before I get any older. Bill wants a family too. Just wish I could get pregnant. I could work till almost time the baby was due. There, I remembered to say almost all my I's instead of aw," Lillian said feeling proud of herself.

I think Charlie's English lessons is really helping us all, don't you?" Naomer asked "I feel a lot more confident in my speech now, not like such a hillbilly," she laugh.

"Oh, definitely, I don't feel like a hillbilly anymore," Lillian laugh along with Naomer.

"Well, I sure hope you do get pregnant. I know you both would like to have a family and would make excellent parents. Aw prayed all the time aw was with Bo that I wouldn't get in the family way after Charlie was born. And it worked. Maybe you should pray to get in the family way," Naomer told her.

"Maybe so. You poor kid, why didn't ya tell your folks that Bo hit you all the time?" Lillian asked.

"Well if he found out that would a just made him madder and he would a beat me more. And if aw left him, you know how folks look down on divorced women anyhow."

"Aw guess he got what was a coming ta him," Lillian slowly said. Naomer was quiet for awhile, "Yeah, I guess so. But he is Charles Thomas' father. I regret he's dead because of that."

"You know my pa molested me and my older sister when we were little," Lillian told her, as she sat up straight as if it might help her to remember better.

"No, aw didn't know that, Lillian."

"Aw kind of blocked it out of my mind. My sister won't even talk to me about it now. But daddy did some awful things to us at night when Ma and the boys were a sleeping."

"But your pa seemed so quiet and nice mannered," Naomer stated.

"Yeah, but at home he sure wasn't. He was a whoppin or beatin one of us all the time, including ma."

"I'm sorry, Lillian. Here ya are a cousin of mine and I never knew."

"Well, daddy's dead now, rest his soul," Lillian said, as she tilted her head back and closed her eyes. "And ma has a little peace and quiet now."

Bill woke up and rubbed his face and ran his fingers through his hair as he called to Charlie. "Hey Charlie, what did ya make in the sand."

"A sand castle, like the one in my story book."

"Oh that's a nice one," Bill said, "tell you what, if we're still here in Oakland next summer, we'll come back to the beach and I'll help you build a great big one. It's gettin kind of cold now, aw think we's best be going, and aw want to take ya'll by the Golden Gate Bridge on the way home."

Charlie's eyes got big with amazement when they stopped close to the Golden Gate Bridge. It towered vibrantly above the water where the Pacific Ocean meets the San Francisco Bay. "They call it the bridge that couldn't be built" remarked Bill. "Aw hear it cost thirty five million dollars to build it and it was finished on May 27th. Of this year."

"What year is this, Bill?" Asked Charlie.

"Why this is 1937 Charlie. Don't they teach you what year it is in school?"

"Yeah, but aw forgot."

"Well, ain't, I mean isn't that something, thirty five million dollars, my, my," Naomer remarked.

"It looks like it comes up out of nowhere with that fog around it," said Lillian.

"It's 1.7 miles long. Look at it shine, ain't it magnificent?" asked Bill.

"It's magnificent," Charlie said, with his big brown eyes fixed on the bridge.

The months flew by. Thanksgiving was lonely with only the four of them having dinner together, when they had all been use to their large families back home on the holidays. For Christmas Bill had a telephone installed in their apartment as a gift to Lillian and Naomer. It was a wall phone and to make a call you had to go through central, which was an operator at the main office. The phone was on a party line with seven other apartment customers on it. Sometimes they would gently pick the phone up and listen to the other parties talking on the line.

Naomer's family in Alabama didn't have a telephone, so she wrote them a letter telling her folks to be at the country grocery store at four o'clock on December 24th to get her call. There was alot of static on the line which was a long way from California to Alabama.

"Ma, is that you, Ma?" Naomer hollered over the line.

"Yes, Darlin, it's me, and Pa and Willer Mae is here a trying to hear ya too. Talk louder. Merry Christmas, Darlin, we all miss you and Charles Thomas so very much. Aw wish ya were both here,"

"Oh Ma, ya'll should see San Francisco and Oakland. They call it the Bay Area. It's so big with the skyscrapers and the ocean, and Ma ya should see the trolley cars. It's all a sight to behold. Ya just wouldn't believe it. But me and Charles Thomas miss ya all so much too. Especially since Christmas is here."

"Ah know," Mae Rosie chocked back her tears. "Now here's ya Pa" "Hi sweetheart."

"Merry Christmas, Pa. Did ja git our package?"

"Sure did, hon, but we're a waiting to open it till tomorrow. Did ya git ourn's?"

"It's under the tree, Pa. I been a trying to keep Charles Thomas from opening it till Christmas. He's excited about Christmas."

"Ah love ya and Charles Thomas and tell Lillian and Bill we all wish them a Merry Christmas to. Now here's Willer Mae."

"Hi, sis," Willer Mae said, "Aw wish you and Charles Thomas were here right now, ah miss ya so much."

"Aw know. Willer Mae honey, we miss ya all so much too. Wait till ya see what we sent you for Christmas, you'll like it ah think. Lillian and Bill send their love to ya'll. Tell the rest of the family we love them too. Am a gonna put Charles Thomas on now, sis. He's been a beggin to call ya'll."

"Hi, Willer Mae, what ya'll been doing?"

"Just a waitin for Christmas. What ya been doing?" She asked.

"Going to school. The teacher made Momma send me to a speech therapist."

"Well Junebugs, Charles Thomas, there ain't nothin wrong with your'n speech."

"Ah know. Momma told them it was because we was from the South and aw had my two front teeth out."

"Here's Granny," Willer Mae told him, and handed the phone to Mae Rosie who was trying to hurry Willer Mae. "Hi Grandson, are ya a waiting for Santa to come?"

"Yes, Mame, aw asked him for a big wagon and a puppy. But Momma says aw can't have a puppy in the city and have ta wait till we move to the country."

"Aw love you, Charles Thomas. Be good and say your prayers ever night. Now here's your granddaddy."

"Hi son, Merry Christmas."

"Merry Christmas, Granddaddy."

"What is Santa bringing ya?"

"A big wagon, aw can haul things in."

"Am a gona hand the phone back to Grandma, so put your momma back on the line."

Mae Rosie's voice crackled and she sounded like she was ready to cry when she repeated," we'ns love ya'll. Say your prayers, Darlin, and have a wonderful Christmas."

"Goodby Ma, we love ya'll too," Naomer told her, and hung the phone gently back on the wall hook. She put her arms around Charlie, and they cried softly together.

The winter was much milder in the Bay area than what Naomer and the others had been used to in Alabama. Spring came early with the beauty of the clear blue skies overhead. The Almond, Cherry and other flowering trees covered the landscape with pink and white blossoms.

Charlie liked school and the city a little better than when they had first came there, but he still longed to move to the country and have a dog and a horse someday. He liked his speech therapist, who was a young man in his early thirties. His speech was improving considerably, and he helped his mother and Lillian and Bill by catching their bad language when he was with them.

Naomer had stayed with her job through the winter, but she was under a lot of pressure at times, especially when the men in the audience got a little out of hand and tried to get on stage with the women or hollered obscenities. Often she was called in on her night off because one of the women got sick and couldn't work. Lou and Joe were nice to her as long as she wasn't late and didn't miss any work nights. When they started a new show with new dance routines she had to come in four hours a day to practice. She was asked out a lot by the men customers, but very seldom did she meet someone she wanted to date.

Bill brought a young truck driver home for dinner several times and he and Naomer started dating in late spring. Bill and Lillian liked him a lot and hoped it would work into a permanent relationship for him and Naomer. Charlie also liked him, and even asked his mother if she might marry Jake someday.

"I think he might make a good dad, don't ya think so too, Momma?" he asked.

"Well, I spose Charlie. But he's not said a thing about marriage, so don't ya go puttin the horse before the cart. Da ya hear, Charlie? Now go outside and get some fresh air," his mother told him.

Lillian put an apron on and patted her stomach which was starting to bulge with a new life that her and Bill were so excited about. "Would ya marry him if he ask ya?" She asked Naomer.

"I don't know. I do like him a lot though, and he would make a good father for Charlie. He has asked me to move way up in the mountains, up by Sonora where his folks live. But he's gone from home so much on the truck it might not work out."

"Did he mention marriage when he asked ya to move way up there?" Lillian asked. "No, he just said he knew Charlie and I didn't care for the city, and we might like it there where it's quiet and peaceful. Not near as many people live there, and everyone knows everybody. Probably about like Guntersville," Naomer answered while sitting the table.

Jake talked Naomer into taking a weekend off from her job and going with him to Sonora to visit his parents. And of course Charlie was invited to go also. Jake had told them all over dinner what the quint little romantic towns were like in the foothills and up into the mountain country. This was the gold rush country, and he said these were very active bustling towns during that time.

Charlie sat between his mother and Jake in the big truck that Jake drove all over the United States hauling loads. He had never been in a truck this big before and was excited that he could see so much more than he could in a car.

Naomer looked over at Jake as he shifted the gears going through towns to get out on the open highway leading to the foothills. Jake was taller that her, maybe close to six feet she thought. He had light brown hair with waves through it and nice facial features on a slender body. He had no more than just kissed her lightly a few times, and a shock ran through her body as she thought what it would be like to make love to him.

"This is the beginning of gold rush country," he told her as they went through the first small town of Jamestown. "These quint little towns have legends, ghost stories and romance in them."

"Oh, you do make them sound alive and exciting," Naomer smiled at him than gazed out the truck window at the old buildings, most of them built back in the gold rush days. The main part through town was only about two city blocks long or less.

They had been on the road for seven hours and Charlie had slept for the last hour, but was beginning to stir in between them. "Where are we?" he asked sitting up straight and rubbing his eyes. "We're almost there, Charlie. Just a few more miles to go," answered Jake. "Sonora is the next little town where my parents live. Tomorrow we'll drive to Columbia,

Angels Camp and Murphys. They're all about alike, but I would like for you to see them. Someday when they have better roads and highways up here I think the towns will be tourist attractions, maybe thirty years from now."

"Look, Charlie, look down into the canyons below," Naomer told him. "These mountains are pretty steep and look at all the beautiful pine trees covering the terrain."

"Oh, that's a long way down to the bottom!" exclaimed Charlie.

"This is God's country," Jake added.

"Yes, it is beautiful, no doubt about that," Naomer answered.

"Sonora was a Mexican camp at one time," Jake begin, "They settled along the southern strip of the Sierra foothills and found gold in abundance. They named Sonora after their hometown province in Mexico. Than the gold rush came along and racial problems started. The average yankee miner disliked and distrusted 'greasers' as they called them. That name 'greasers' was actually written into some laws back then," Jake went on, "Well, the Mexicans or Chilenos were more experienced in mining and did far better than the greenhorn Americans which led to a Foreign Miner's tax law in 1850, that imposed a fee of twenty dollars a month to all miners of foreign birth."

"Gosh, did ya learn all that history in school?" asked Charlie.

"Some of it. I love this country," Jake said with pride in his voice. "I know I'm not here much, being on the truck driving all over the country, but this is home and I always run back to it when I can."

"Oh, it is beautiful up here and so peaceful and quiet," Naomer said, "Do you like it, Charlie?"

"Yep! It sure is better than Oakland," Charlie mused while they both laugh.

When they arrived at Jake's parent's home both his mother and father came out to greet them. After all the introductions, Mrs. Ullman put her arm around Naomer and they walked up the narrow sidewalk to the small white house with brown shutters. Jake grabbed the two suitcases, and Mr.Ullmand held Charlie's hand while they walked toward the house.

"How old are you, Charlie?" he asked, limping a little from an old injury as they walked along.

"Almost six years old, sir. I'm in the first grade at Washington Grammar School."

"I bet that's a great big school there in the big city where you live," Mr. Ullman said.

"Yes sir. There's thirty five kids just in my class."

"Oh that is a big classroom of kids," he said, as they followed the women through the front door and into a small living room with a couch and several overstuffed chairs setting close to the fireplace.

"It's so cozy in here," remarked Naomer, "Ya have a fire going."

"Yes, it still gets a little bit cold up here until around the end of May, so we keep a small fire going all time," answered Mrs. Ullman, while taking the poker and stirring the fire around to get more heat. "We're so glad you could come up with Jake. He's been telling us so much about you and Charlie," she said putting the poker back in place.

"Well, thank ya. We enjoyed the ride. Charlie slept some of the way here," Naomer said and smoothed Charlie's hair down while he stood with his hands toward the fireplace to warm them.

"I'd tell you to sit down, but I guess you're all tired of sitting after that long trip clear from Oakland. I have supper ready so I'll just sit the table and we'll eat."

After supper Mrs. Ullman showed Naomer and Charlie the guest bedroom where they would sleep. "Our chesterfield makes into a bed and Jake will be comfortable there." They all sat around the fireplace and visited the rest of the evening, after Jake and Naomer did the dishes and Mrs. Ullman put the leftovers away.

On the way back to Oakland several days later, Naomer cuddled up to Jake, while Charlie slept in the small sleeper behind them. It was beginning to get dark, and Jake turned his headlights on than put his arm around Naomer. "Well, what did you think about those little mountain towns, Babe?" he asked.

"Oh, aw loved them. The fresh air smells so good and small home town atmosphere is just like home, maybe even better. And your folks are so nice."

"I could have Mom look for you a house to rent. What if I paid part of the rent, than when I was home I would stay there too."

"Aw think I would like that," She smiled at him and kissed him on the cheek. "Do ya think I could find a good waitress job there?"

"Sure, I know the owner of the restaurant just out of town. I'll call him. Should make pretty good tips there. A lot of logging truckers stop there."

Charlie would love to live up there, and maybe he could have a puppy. He wants one so bad." "I might be able to take care of that too," he smiled and she cuddled closer.

Just can't believe you're really moving up in the mountains to the gold rush country, Naomer," Lillian said, while they were doing the dishes after supper.

"Jake's mother found us a two bedroom older home with a fenced in yard and all, and some used furniture too. She's loaning me a set of her old dishes and pots and pans. Her and Jake's dad are sure nice people."

"What do they say about Jake staying with ya when he comes home?" Lillian asked with a worried note in her voice.

"They don't know it yet. I reckon he'll tell them though," Naomer answered.

"Has he ever mentioned marriage yet?" Lillian asked.

"No, but I think he will soon. But I don't know if aw really want ta marry him. I really like him, but I just don't think am ready to marry again. Not yet anyhow," Naomer answered.

"Well honey, in a small mountain town there's bound to be talk if he lives there some of the time, and ya know there's only one reason a man wants to live with a woman." Lillian usually says what was on her mind. Naomer knew Lillian didn't want her to get hurt later and was telling her this for her own good, but she tended to ignore her statement.

"Lillian, I'll come back and stay with you awhile when you have the baby. Should be about August, shouldn't it?" she asked, not waiting for Lillian to answer. "Maybe Charlie won't have started the new school year yet."

"Well, aw, I mean I appreciate that. But we'll see how your new job is by then. Ya might not be able to take off work, and if the baby comes late we don't want Charlie to miss any school. We'll see."

"He'll finish school here in June before we all leave, and if he has to start late there in second grade, it won't hurt. Now don't ya, I mean don't you worry about it," Naomer told her. They were both trying to stop saying aw for I and ya for you, trying to speak correct English, but sometimes it was hard to remember with so many other things on their mind.

"I feel responsible for ya comin to California, so don't you go off gettin into trouble up there in them mountains, da ya hear?" Lillian said half jokingly. "Your Ma and Pa would be after my hide if something happened to you."

"Well, I'm over twenty one now, so no ones responsible for me, but me, and ya just tell Ma that if she gets mad."

"Aw know you're your own boss, but I'm older then you and I just feel responsible in a way. Come here, honey." Lillian hugged her close, "Me and Bill love ya and Charlie, and we're sure gonna miss the two of you." They both laugh because Lillian's stomach was getting so big it was in the way.

Naomer backed away and looked at her, "I'm just thrilled that you and Bill are a startin your family. I hope the first ones a boy so's he can take of the others. And you're gonna need that other bedroom for a nursery.

"Now just hold on there a second, how many do you think am a gonna have?" Lillian asked her smiling.

"Oh, thought ya might have four or five at least?"

"No not over three, I hope. I'm gonna send Bill to the doctor."

"Oh, ho, ho, and what's Bill gonna say about that?"

"Well, if he don't want ta feed a bunch of kids, he better go."

Naomer studied for awhile, "I guess that is the only way to take care of that," she said, as she hung the tea towel over the cabinet door and took her starched apron off, hanging it on a nail on the side of the cabinet. "Too bad they don't discover a pill a woman could just take and she wouldn't get pregnant."

"Oh, I spose that will be sometime way in the future, if ever, honey," answered Lillian. "The good Lord just wants this here world populated or he would of had some way for us to keep from getting pregnant.

When Naomer had time off from her job, she and Charlie went with Jake again up to Sonora. Charlie missed two days of school, but at the end of the school year they didn't do much. Naomer wanted to learn the way up there better before she drove the long drive herself. They looked at a house that Jake's mother had found for her to rent, and went to talk to the owner of the restaurant that Jake knew, and about the waitress job he had already inquired about. Both the job and the house were better than Naomer had expected, and Charlie was thrilled to be moving to the mountains and out of the big city.

Lou and Joe were both upset with Naomer for leaving the dance hall. She was one of their best dancers, and special customers came to watch her more than any of the other girls in the course line. "Why don't ya make a career of dancing, Doll? There's good moola in it," Lou said to her in his broken Italian.

"Guess the theatre is not in my blood, Lou. Too much night life for me. I need to be with Charlie at night, and Jake when he's home," she told him.

"Well Kid, it's been nice knowing ya and I hope you like that new restaurant job. If not, you always have a place here," Lou told her as he hugged her and walked away to his office.

Naomer liked her new job and worked four days a week and two evenings. Mrs. Ullman kept Charlie on the evenings she worked. Charlie liked it at the Ullmans and tried to be on his best behavior at all times. Mrs. Ullman was a good cook and he enjoyed her Beef Stroganoff and pies and cakes. Mr. Ullman let Charlie help him pick the tomatoes, radishes, onions and other vegetables from their garden and let him help with the weeding, after he showed him the difference between the vegetables leaves and the weeds. Charlie mistakingly picked the wrong thing a couple of times, but soon knew the difference.

His favorite place was in the branches of an old Apple tree in the Ullman's backyard, where he had been warned not to climb to high. Charlie called it his 'grandma tree' because whenever he was worried about anything he climbed up in the branches of the old tree and told her his problem. "I'm worried about a startin a new school with all new kids I have ta meet," he told her. "I like this town and these here mountains, but aw sure wish aw had a brother to go ta school with, or at least a puppy aw could play with when I got home from School."

"Charlie, come into lunch now," Mrs. Ullman hollered out the back door, knowing he was in the old Apple tree.

"Yes Mame, I'm a comin," he answered, as he climbed down two branches than jumped to the ground below. Hot beef stew was steaming in bowls on the table and homemade bread with hand churned butter, and honey from Mr. Ullman's bee hives. "Umm sure looks good, Mame, and smells delicious. Wish my Momma made good stuff like this."

"Well now Charlie, your mother works hard at that restaurant and doesn't have time to cook very much. She probably brings food home sometimes from the restaurant."

"Yes Mame, she brings home fried Chicken and mashed potatoes and gravy a lot. But none of it tastes as good as your cookin."

"Well thanks Charlie," Mrs. Ullman said and winked at her husband.

"Charlie, what say, we go a fishing this afternoon," Mr. Ullman stated, "over to the creek. I hear they been a catching some big ones there."

"Oh can we?" Charlie asked excited. "Ya know, ya both are just like my grandma and grandpa Green in Alabama. Aw sure miss them, but having ya'll sure helps when aw miss them."

Summer continued to go by. Charlie met a boy his age that lived a few houses from the Ullmans. Kenny and Charlie had become good friends and was anxious to start second grade together in September. Kenny stayed over night with Charlie twice and Charlie stayed over night at Kenny's once through the summer. They played in the woods together and built forts to play cowboys and Indians and cops and robbers. Mr. Ullman help them make stick horses for their mounts, and police cars out of wooden crates. He also put up an old tent he had, in the backyard for the boys to play in when Charlie was there.

Naomer and Jake talked of getting married, but neither seemed to want to commit themselves. Jake continued sleeping at his folk's home when he was there, but spent the days and evenings with Naomer and Charlie.

Naomer liked waitressing and enjoyed talking with the customers. The truckers were all polite and some of them asked her for dates, but she felt committed to Jake for now. There was a telephone at the restaurant and she wrote her family in Alabama and told them what day and time to call her, as they still had no telephone. She had Charlie at the restaurant when they called so he could talk to them also.

In late August the phone rang while Naomer was cleaning the restaurant to close for the night. The owner answered, as he was closer to the phone, working on the next day's menu. "For you Naomer."

"Hello."

"I'm a proud daddy. Lillian just had a eight pound, two ounce baby boy," Bill announced.

"She did," Naomer squealed, "Oh congratulations Bill! A boy, just what ya both wanted."

"Yup, a big healthy boy. Kinda looks like me to."

"Well, how long will Lillian be in the hospital? I'll ask my boss for three or four days off, and come to help her when she comes home," Naomer said.

"They'll keep her there about four days, I reckon," answered Bill.

"Hold on a minute, Bill, the boss is right here." Naomer talked to her boss who agreed she could take four days off to go to Oakland. "Okay Bill, I'll be there in a few days."

Naomer and Charlie were both excited about seeing the new baby, and Lillian and Bill also, as they had not seen them since they moved to the mountains. They left before daylight and arrived in Oakland about noon. Naomer prayed that her old car that Jake had found for her to buy, would make it over the Altamont Mountains without any trouble.

Bill had just brought Lillian and the new baby home from the hospital and put them in bed when Naomer and Charlie got there. Naomer kissed Bill on the cheek before hurrying into the bedroom with Charlie on her heels. "Oh Lillian, he's a handsome fellow. Oh look at that dimple just like Bills," she giggled.

"What did ya'll name him?" Charlie inquired.

William Charles," after you and Bill," Lillian smiled, knowing Charlie would be delighted.

"Really. He has my name too," Charlie grinned.

"Yap, but we'll call him Billy, so's we don't get ya'll three mixed up when we're a talking about ya," Lillian answered.

Naomer gave the baby his bath the next morning while Charlie watched attentively. Bill had gone to work, and Lillian sat in a chair in her housecoat trying to regain her strength so she could take over when Naomer went back to the mountains.

"I wish he was big enough to play with," Charlie said as the baby looked at him wide eyed, while Naomer cuped water over him with the palm of her hand.

"Oh, I reckon he'll be big afore we know it," she answered.

"When will you have a baby, Momma, so's we can have one at home?"

Lillian giggled, and Naomer said, "well, ya have to be married first, Charlie."

"Why don't ya and Jake get married. Then ya could stay home and not have to work."

Lillian giggled again, louder this time "He's serious, the boy knows what he's talking about."

"Oh shut up Lillian. Maybe someday, Charlie, not right now," answered his mother.

Several weeks after they returned to the mountains Charlie started school. The children were friendlier at the country school than they were in the city. The little girl who sat at the desk in front of Charlie took a liking to him and turned around smiling a toothless smile every few minutes. Her name was Marsha. She had long blond pig tails that got dipped in the ink wells on the desk every time a little boy got a chance. Most of the time the ends of her pig tails were purple from the ink.

Kenny was still Charlie's best friend, and they played with several other children in town after school. Their favorite games were 'Ante Ante Over', 'Red Rover', and 'Hide n Go Seek'. Charlie enjoyed his mother's days off from work and helped her clean house, bake cookies or go for a walk around the little town.

"Momma, remember the story Jake told us about Sonora?" Charlie asked. "Well, we're studying the history of it in school, and did ya know during the gold rush days for entertainment on Sunday afternoons the miners would fight a bear and a bull together? Around a six hundred pound grizzly bear, Momma, was chained to either his pen or the bull. The mean men poked them with spears to make them mad so's they would fight each other."

"Oh Charlie, that's gruesome," Naomer told him.

"Yeah, the more blood they saw, the more the men cheered," Charlie went on. "One time there was about two thousand people there and the wounded bull jumped the fence and ran wild in the crowd of people and gored one man to death and trampled some others. And then," he said, "A man decided to throw some hot water on the bear, and the bear grabbed him and chewed him up. They shot the bear."

"Oh, how horrible. They shouldn't be teaching that to little kids in school," his mother told him.

"Well, it's history, Momma."

Naomer had an early shift at the restaurant and woke Charlie early to take him to the Ullmans before he went to school. She found a note on the door saying Mrs. Ullman had become ill through the night and had to go to the hospital. Naomer took Charlie to the restaurant and gave him some breakfast and told him to read in his reader until she could get away to take him to school.

Also when she got a chance she called the hospital to see how Mrs. Ullman was. She was told it was her heart and she would be in the hospital for several days. Naomer thought it may be best if she found someone else to watch Charlie for awhile. She was afraid the anxiety of a small child would be too much for Mrs. Ullman with a bad heart.

She inquired with her customers that afternoon. A sheriff that lived in town said his wife would take care of Charlie. She would have to pay more for Charlie to stay at the Grahans, but she was determined to make ends meet. Charlie was sad that he couldn't stay with the Ullmans anymore. They had become like grandparents to him and taken the place of his grandparents in Alabama.

"Mrs. Ullman ain't going to die is she Momma?" Charlie asked tearfully.

"No Charlie, but the strain of watching a little boy might be just too much for her now. And don't say ain't anymore, say isn't. We both need to start using better English."

"But am good at the Ullmans, Momma. I even help her some with house work and help Mr. Ullman in the garden."

"You'll like it at Officer's Grahan's house, he has a son just three years older than you that goes to your school. Ya can walk to school with him on days I have ta drop you off early."

Charlie and Denzil Grahan didn't hit it off to well. Denzil was nine years old and spoiled rotten by his mother. He didn't want another boy getting any of the attention of his parents, and let it be known to Charlie to watch his step, and not be too friendly with his mother or father or he would beat him up on the way home from school.

About three weeks after Charlie started staying with the Grahans, he, Denzil and some of the neighborhood children, mostly Denzil's friends, were playing baseball at the end of the street. Denzil was up at bat and swung hard hitting the ball into a neighbor's front window. The kids all ran away before the owner of the house came outside. That evening the owner took the ball to Officer Grahan and told him what happened. Denzil blamed the broken window on Charlie, and Officer Grahan lectured Charlie the next day about hitting balls toward houses and running away afterwards instead of owning up to it. He told Charlie he had to stay in after school and do homework for a whole week and his mother would have to pay for the window. Charlie told his mother all about the broken window incident, and the next evening when she picked Charlie up she was still upset about it.

"Now Naomer, my son wouldn't lie about it. He said Charlie broke the window and I believe him. He ain't got no reason to lie to me," Officer Grahan told her.

"What about the other kids that saw it. Did ya ask any of them what happened?" she ask.

"No need to. Denzil has never lied to me and he ain't about to start. Now your gonna have ta pay for that window."

"Well, Charlie's never lied to me neither, and aw ain't about to pay for any winder my boy didn't break," Naomer hotly told him. "And I guess he won't be a comin back to your house anymore. Your son has been mean to him since he first started staying with ya," she said, while opening her purse and taking out a twenty dollar bill. "Now here's for the rest of the days aw owe ya for," she said, as she threw the money at him and stomped out the door. "Come on Charlie, we're not welcomed here."

"You'll be sorry for this," he hollered after her.

A few days later Naomer received a call at work from a juvenile delinquent officer from Stockton telling her that he needed to make an appointment with her and Charlie as a complaint had been turned in against her. The complaint said that Charlie should be taken away from her and placed in a children's detention home as he was out of control, and Naomer being single and working so much didn't take proper care of him.

Naomer was ready for the appointment with the juvenile delinquent officer when he arrived. He was an older grey headed man with a pleasant appearance and carried a brief case.

"Come in Mr. Black, sir, and please sit down."

"As I told you on the phone, Mrs. Parker, we had a complaint from a sheriff's officer here in town," he said, as he opened his brief case taking out a pad and pencil.

"Yes sir, Officer Grahan I imagine." Naomer went on to tell him her and Charlie's story and then called Charlie from his bedroom where he was playing, to tell his part of it.

"Please don't make me leave my Momma," Charlie pleaded, "Aw didn't do anything bad."

"Well son, I believe you and your mother," Mr. Black said and patted Charlie on the shoulder. "We've had other complaints about Officer Grahan. I'll recommend that you stay at home with your mother. But Mrs. Parker try to find a suitable baby sitter during your working hours. I may not be able to help you if we get another complaint. But otherwise I don't think you'll hear anymore about this matter."

"Thank you, sir," Naomer said.

"Thank you, sir," Charlie echoed.

Mrs. Ullman had heard the gossip around town about the incident with the Grahans and called Naomer to tell her she would be more than happy to watch Charlie until she could find a good sitter. So Charlie was happy once more that he got to go back to stay with his pretend grandparents. Naomer heard no more from the Stockton office, but knew Officer Grahan was spreading stories around town about her and also saying Jake lived with her when he was in town.

Business had fallen off at the restaurant and her boss was complaining about it being so slow. "Naomer, you're a real good worker and I know this isn't your fault, but I'm gonna have to let you go. I'm really sorry and I hope this restaurant experience will help you find another good job," he said while rubbing his bald head. "Somebody should kick that Grahan's butt for all the trouble he's caused. But who's gonna go against a sheriff."

"Pete, I was afraid it was comin to this. I've really enjoyed working here, but aw don't blame you, the restaurant has to stay busy. I'll probably have to move to another town," she said.

She stayed at the restaurant another few days and also looked for another job around town, but felt that Officer Grahan had ruined her reputation in town and hurt the Ullmans too with his vicious lies.

Jake came home, and after she told him all that had happened he was mad enough to bust Officer Grahan in the nose. "No Jake, that wouldn't help and it would just cause more heartache for your folks. And Lord knows we don't want your mother to have a heart attack. It's just best if Charlie and me move to another town or go back to Oakland," Naomer assured him.

"Well, I'll help you get another job and help with expenses until you find something. Murphys is a bigger town maybe something will be open there."

It didn't take Naomer long to get another restaurant job with the letter of recommendation that her boss Pete had wrote for her. The Murphy's Hotel was one of the largest and oldest hotels and restaurants in the mountain area. It was a luxury hotel on Main Street built in 1854 by James Sperry, Naomer was told, and was named Sperry and Perry Hotel when it was first built, but was destroyed by fire in 1859 and rebuilt more elegant than ever. Later it acquired the name Murphy's Hotel.

Naomer had to work more hours, but her tips were far better than at the other restaurant, because of the richer clientele. The only problem was Charlie. With all the evening hours she had to work it seemed the only solution was to board him with a family and bring him home on her days off. She hated to do that, but they would have to go back to Oakland otherwise, and Charlie said he would rather be boarded out then to go back to the big city.

Naomer ran an ad in the town newspaper, where as an older lady answered it saying she was a widow and she would like to have a little boy's company, and she badly needed the income. Charlie seemed to like the lady whose name was Sara Mitchell. She lived close to the school in Murphys so Charlie could walk to school, and Naomer could visit anytime she wanted. Naomer had found a small one bedroom house to live in, and her and Charlie shared the bed when he was home. He loved to cuddle up to his mother especially in the cold fall weather that they were now having.

The holidays were approaching fast and Charlie was excited about Christmas coming. Lillian had called the restaurant where Naomer worked and invited them to come to Oakland for Thanksgiving, but Naomer had to work on the holiday, and Mrs.Mitchell had planned to cook a late evening thanksgiving dinner for them after Naomer got off. Jake was home for the holiday and was invited also.

Snow was on the ground the middle of December which promised a white Christmas. The days were cold and it was Charlie's job to bring in the wood for the fireplace. He missed his mother a lot, but the week went by quite fast until her two days off. He was going to be in the Christmas play at school and begged his mother to come to it.

"Of course I'll come to your play. I'll get one of the other waitress' to exchange days with me, so I can go. She picked up Charlie and Mrs. Mitchell, who had become like one of the family, and drove the short distant to the school.

The children were excited and running around while the teachers were trying to get them in place for the first play to begin. The play was about a poor family and a rich old man who was mean, but had a change of heart and bought them all Christmas presents at the end. Charlie had a part as one of the little boys, and also recited a poem after the play was over. He still had some of his southern accent and the audience laugh at his words. But it was a laugh of acceptance and they clapped for him because he was cute and funny at the same time. Santa arrived at the end of the program and gave bags of candy and oranges to everyone.

"I haven't had this much fun in ages," Mrs. Mitchell remarked on the way back to her house. "I really enjoyed that play and Santa Clause. The spirit of Christmas is so fulfilling."

"Yes, aw enjoyed it too. Charlie and I don't get away to have much fun lately. Seems like I just work all the time now. Aw appreciate the fact that Charlie has you for his grandmother now," Naomer said, as she pulled into Mrs. Mitchell's driveway.

"Oh, I just love this little boy," Mrs. Mitchell said as she hugged Charlie who was sitting between them. He brings so much happiness into my life. My grandchildren live a long ways from here and I hardly ever get to see them."

The purple and yellow wild flowers covered the hills and mountains that spring. The deer were plentiful and Charlie saw some quite often. He even saw a bear and cub about a quarter mile from the edge of town.

Charlie was still waiting for a puppy, but since he was boarded with Mr. Mitchell most of the time, the puppy would have to stay home alone, so Naomer thought it best to wait until he was older before they got one. But as things turned out Jake called and said he had a surprise for them and would be over that evening. It happened to be Naomer's day off, so she cooked a pot roast with potatoes and carrots and cleaned the house till it was spotless. Charlie helped too, while he tried to guess what Jake's surprise was. He knew it was not a puppy because they had all discussed that and decided it would be too hard to have one with them both gone so much.

A loud knock at the door sent Charlie racing to open it, knowing Jake would be there with some kind of surprise. Charlie gasp when he saw a little black face with rust markings in Jake's arms.

"A puppy for me?" he asked.

"Now who else do you think this pup would be for?" Jake asked, while handing the pup to Charlie. The puppy snuggled up to Charlie licking his freckled face and ears while Charlie giggled.

"Oh a puppy," Naomer said as she came into the living room from the kitchen. "Jake you didn't. I thought we had discussed this."

"Well, this is a Rottweiler. A rare breed here in the states now. The parents come from Germany. She was the runt of the litter and I got her cheaper because of that, but she'll make a fine dog someday. The man I bought her from in New York said this breed had only been here in United States since about 1929. About ten years now. There is one restriction. The man said she cannot be bred to any other breed of dog, only another Rottweiler to keep the breed pure. Charlie probably won't want to raise any puppies, and I doubt if another Rottweiler could be found in the state of California, so we'll have her spayed when she's a little older."

"Ya brought her clear from New York? The state of New York?" Naomer asked in disbelief.

"Yes Mame, I read this article in the newspaper there while I was waiting for my truck to be loaded and it sounded like such a fine breed of dog that I called the man that owned some, and he had this one little female left that hadn't sold yet. Said it would grow up to be just as big as the others in the litter."

"How in the world did'ja travel clear across the United States with a little puppy?" Naomer asked still in disbelief.

"It wasn't easy, but she's three months old now and she soon learned to relieve herself only when she got out of the truck. I had to stop a lot more than I normally do, but we made it here. These are very intelligent dogs, maybe the smartest breed alive," Jake sounded as though he was trying to sell a set of encyclopedias and the lady maybe didn't want them. "Well you do want her don't ya?" he asked.

"Aw love her already," Charlie said hugging the puppy close while she washed his face again, wiggling her short stubby tail which had been docked short.

"Of course, Jake. Aw just can't believe ya went to all that trouble to get Charlie a puppy when there's plenty of free one around here".

"But not like this one," Jake said. "She's special just like Charlie. I made her a big dog house today, so when she has to stay outside she'll have her own house. And I'm going to fix your fence so she can't get out of the yard. She's too valuable to get lost. She'll be a good watch dog for you when she grows up and they are very protective dogs.

"Jake, you're special too. What would we do without you," Naomer said, and kissed him on the cheek.

"Well, if you think I'm so special, why don't ya marry me than?" he asked, putting his arms around her waist.

"We'll see, maybe later. I don't have time to get married. They keep me so darn busy down at that restaurant, all I want to do when I come home is sleep. Now how can I be a house wife and sleep all the time when am home?"

"You can quit working, Babe. I make enough money for all of us to live nicely."

"But I just got my independence when aw moved out here to California, and I'm making good money now," Naomer said, forgetting her correct English and becoming flustered at Jake's persistence of marriage lately. Aw don't know, Jake, just give me a little more time. Now I bet you're starved so I'll go get supper on the table," she said and hurried off toward the kitchen, leaving Charlie to keep Jake company.

"What would you like to name your pup, Charlie? Do you have any ideas?" asked Jake.

"Well, I think I'll call her Venture. That's a new word aw just learned. And she ventured all the way here from New York. And that's further than Alabama, Momma says."

"Hey, that's a good name. Venture."

The following week was hectic with spring banquets and dinner meetings at the restaurant. Naomer was working nine hours a day. Split shifts from mid morning till early afternoons, and than supper hours to late evening hours. Sometimes she had to bar tend if the restaurant was slow and the bar was full.

A movie crew from Hollywood was in town to set up for a movie to be filmed in Murphys, and they were staying at the Murphy's Hotel. The waitresses were all bussing about the movie crew and the movie to be filmed, not to speak of the movie stars that would be coming into town. They were told there would be plenty of jobs for extras, and any one could apply.

"What do ya spose this movie is about?" Naomer asked Karen, one of the other waitresses, as they were cleaning up for the night.

"Probably the Gold Rush. This is where it happened," Karen answered, as she stopped folding napkins and brushed her curly blond hair back from her face.

"Naomer, you're wanted on the telephone. Long distant," the restaurant manager hollered to her. "Hello."

"Naomer, this is your Pa." his voice sounded strange, as though he had been crying.

"Daddy, what's wrong. Something's wrong."

"Honey," he cried, "We lost your Ma tonight."

"What, what do ya mean, ya lost Ma tonight, Daddy?"

"It was her heart, Darlin. It just quit working."

"No, Pa, tell me it ain't true. Not Ma, no no, she screamed loudly and the manager took the phone and reassured Pa that he would take care of Naomer.

Karen took her in the back room and put her arms around her trying to comfort her while she cried and screamed over and over, "no, no, not Ma, it can't be true."

"Karen, can you take her on home and stay with her? I'll finish your work here," the manager told her.

"Yeah, sure. I think she could use a good stiff drink too before we go home. I'll take her by the restaurant bar,"

"Okay, but I don't think she's use to drinking too much," he said.

Karen helped Naomer undress, as she was still in a state of shock, and put her to bed making sure she was asleep before she left the house. The drinks had calmed her and made her sleep.

In the early morning hours Naomer dreamed her and Ma were holding hands running through a field of wild flowers, but they didn't see the drop off in front of them and Ma fell over it on to a ledge below. She tried to reach Ma's hand, and Ma reached toward her but they couldn't grasp each other. She tried over and over again to reach her, but couldn't. Naomer woke up in a cold sweat and death of her mother surfaced to her brain and over powered everything else.

"Momma, Momma, I love you," she cried. "Why did I leave you," she repeated over and over again. She finally got up and showered and fixed herself a cut of hot strong coffee. She called Lillian in Oakland and told her about Momma.

"Do you want us to come over there, Hon?" Lillian asked "Or why don't you and Charlie come stay here for awhile."

"I can't get away from the restaurant right now, Lillian, it's a busy time and there's a big movie crew here from Hollywood. They're going to be making a movie and they'll be here for months. Even if you came over here I wouldn't have any time to visit with you right now. Aw really think workin will keep my mind off of Momma better."

I spose you're right, Hon," Lillian answered and they talked some more about the baby and Charlie before hanging up.

Karen picked Naomer up to take her to the restaurant as they had left Naomer's car there last night. She talked to the manager to see if she could take a couple days off and he had already made arrangements for one of the other waitresses to fill in for her.

"I have to go get my little boy and tell him. Aw know he's a gonna take his grandma's death so hard. Aw dread tellin him," Naomer told Karen and Dean, the manager, while wiping her tears with a tissue.

"Oh, Honey," Karen said, and put her arms around Naomer. Kids take this kind of news better than what you think they do.

"Well, Dear, take a couple of days and spend them with your boy. I'd give you more time off, but you know how strapped we are right now with this movie crew in town," Dean told her and whispered in her ear. "And you know you're my best."

"Aw think it's good I work and keep my mind off momma. I'll see ya'll in two days."

She called Mrs. Mitchell and told her about her mother, and that she would take Charlie home for the two days. Charlie didn't take his grandmother's death as hard as Naomer expected he would. But he was young and being away from her for over a year eased the loss for a young boy. They spent the day together with Venture tagging along. They walked up town and wired some money to Pa and the family to help pay for a blanket wreath for Ma's casket.

Naomer thought about flying back home for the funeral, but she couldn't really afford it, and she was afraid she might not want to come back to California if she went. No this was her's and Charlie's home now. There was no place back in Alabama for her—no work, no nothing, except for her family. But they were all married now and had families of their own, except for Willer Mae who was almost grown and would soon be out of high school. There was enough of the family there to take care of Pa and Willer Mae.

"We won't ever get to see Grandma Mae Rosie again, will we Momma?' Charlie asked, with his big brown eyes wide with wonder.

"Someday in Heaven we'll see her again, Charlie," Naomer answered, while she sat on their lawn drawing with a stick in the dirt where there was no grass, and Charlie pumped himself in the swing Jake had hung up for him in an old Black Walnut Tree.

Venture barked and kept trying to grab Charlie's foot in the swing, and then tried to get the stick that Naomer was drawing with in the dirt. She finally let Venture have it and the young pup ran off to herself to chew on it. Naomer was hesitant at first about having Venture, but it had taught Charlie about responsibility, and she was amazed at how he had taken over with Ventures feeding and brushing and the time consuming problems of raising a puppy. And Mrs. Mitchell was so kind to let Charlie keep Venture at her house when he was there.

Naomer looked at the black sleek coat of the pup and the dark mahogany markings. Her beautiful wide head with the short stop was getting more prominent as she grew. She only hoped this magnificent animal she was becoming, lived to an old age because Charlie was so attached to her already.

"Rottweiler. I wonder where they came up with that name from?" Naomer wondered out loud.

"Didn't you hear Jake say, Momma, that man he bought her from said these dogs come from overseas. Germany I think he said, from uh===a town called Rottweil. But he said they really came from Rome, but the Germans stole two or three and kept them for thousands of years."

"My you do have a memory don't you. Well, am just glad you finally got your puppy."

The sun was bright and warm on them. The leaves were budding out on the tree that held the swing, but didn't yet shade the yard. Naomer wished Jake was here. Maybe she should marry him, he was a very good man. He was back on the road headed for the east coast and would be gone a month this time. Just when she needed him too. He was the only one she could really talk to and bear her soul , except for Lillian, who was too far away in Oakland.

Naomer tried not to cry anymore that day for Charlie's sake, but at times she felt like screaming as loud as she could. She did scream and cry after Charlie went to sleep. She turned their old radio on loud and screamed and cried until she was exhausted and tired enough to sleep.

She needed the closeness of her family now, and the telephone was the only way. She talked to them several times that month. They still did not have a telephone, but she would write and tell them the best time to call her at the restaurant or a specific time she would call the grocery store in Guntersville.

The film crew had started filming the movie and the whole country side came out to watch. A lot of the people were used as extras in the movie. The town was almost as busy as in the Gold Rush days. Charlie was in awe of all the cowboys and horses and bulletless shooting going on. He and his mother dressed up in the old fashion clothing handed out to wear from the movie crew, and were in scenes with groups of people. With the extra money they made Naomer was able to start a small savings account.

After the movie was finally finished and the stars and crew left town, Murphys was almost like a ghost town. It was late summer by than and school would be starting very soon in September.

"Aw wish Venture could go to school with me," Charlie told his mother who was at the sink mixing oatmeal cookie dough on her day off.

"Well son, school's no place for dogs. She probably wouldn't even like it there," Naomer told him as she looked at Charlie who had his cheek laying against Venture's back where she lay on the floor. "My goodness, that dog is almost as big as you are."

"Yap, they weighed her on the feed store scales the other day, Momma, and she weighed fifty five pounds."

"She is getting more beautiful everyday," Naomer said and Venture looked at her with dark wide set eyes, as if she knew what Naomer said. "And protective too. Aw hope she don't bite anyone."

Oh she loves everybody, Momma, specially the kids that come over to play. Aw can't wait for Jake to see her," Charlie said with pride in his voice, as he petted Venture's shoulder while still laying on her.

Jake was expected to be there in early evening for supper. He had been gone another month this time and they were both anxious to see him. Naomer had been having drinks lately with some of the other restaurant employees after work, and had dated several men, which she wasn't anxious to tell Jake about. The drinking seemed to ease the pain of losing her mother, and helped her to sleep when she went home to an empty house.

Jake arrived late because he had mechanical problems with his car between Sonora and Murphys. When he knocked on the door Venture charged toward the door barking protectively to take care of her family. Naomer grabbed her collar before opening the door.

"Hey Venture," Jake said, "you should remember me." Venture immediately started wiggling all over and whining in greeting Jake.

"Ain't she got big, Jake?" was the first thing out of Charlie's mouth.

"Hey she has, and protective too," answered Jake, "But there's no such word as ain't. Try not to use that word."

"Okay, I forget sometimes," answered Charlie. "And she weighs fifty five pounds, don't she mom?"

"That's right," Naomer confirmed, "Charlie had her weighed down at the feed store. We all sure miss you, Jake," Naomer said and kissed him lightly on the mouth. "Bet you're starved. Your late too. Let's all go into the kitchen and I'll put supper on the table."

"I had car problems coming over. Sorry I'm so late. Sure is good to be home. I sure get tired of being out there on the road all time."

It was nine o'clock before they finished supper. Naomer had to order Charlie to wash in the pan of warm water she heated for him and to get ready for bed, while she cleaned the kitchen. Jake took Venture outside for a walk before he helped her finish the dishes.

Charlie and Venture was sent to bed, and Naomer turned the radio on to some soft music before her and Jake relaxed on the couch.

"How are your parents doing, Jake?" she asked.

"Well, Ma's still not feeling very strong. Dad's helping around the house as much as he can. I've been paying a cleaning lady to come in every other week, against their protests, and clean good and do some cooking for them."

"That's thoughtful of you, Jake. I bet they really appreciate that. Aw sure miss my family. My mom especially, knowing aw won't ever see her again, not on earth anyway."

"I'm so sorry, Hon," Jake sympathetically said, "I know I haven't been here much for you."

91

"Well, ya can't help it. Ya have to work." She didn't know how to tell Jake she had dated other men this month. She knew it best to just blurt it out and get it over with, but she didn't want to hurt him. He had always been so good to her and Charlie.

"Jake, I've had a few drinks lately. It helps me ta sleep better since Momma died."

"Just don't let it be habit forming, Hon, drinking is bad for your health."

"I've been lonely lately, and a couple of the waitresses aw work with invited me to have a drink at the restaurant bar after work." She hesitated awhile, "Jake, I've also dated twice with different guys."

Jake didn't say anything for awhile. Naomer wondered what he was thinking–what his reaction would be. "I thought it was understood we were a couple. That we wouldn't date others," he quietly said. "I love you and want to marry you, but evidently you'll never feel the same way," he said as he stood up from the couch and paced around the living room.

"Jake, aw only went to a movie with one guy, and had a few drinks and danced with another fellow at the restaurant bar. I didn't sleep with them. I'm young and lonely and not ready to settle down and marry again. And are you a telling me that you don't go out when you're out on the road."

Jake was silent, still pacing and looking out the front window to the dark street. "No, I don't go out with other women."

"I really care for you," Naomer went on, "aw want to be with you, but I just can't marry you now. I know this don't make sense. Maybe I'm just all mixed up. Please understand."

"I understand you don't really love me enough or you would want to marry me," Jake said in anger. Maybe I better just walk out of your life because I don't want to be hurt anymore. We've been going together for over a year and you should know by now whether you really love me enough to marry me or not. And I guess you don't ." Jake grabbed his jacket and left out the door.

"Jake wait, please don't be angry," Naomer hollered, as Jake got in his car and drove off. She sat back down on the couch and buried her head in her hands. Why did she have to hurt Jake. He was such a good friend. Why did he have to be so serious. She was glad Charlie was asleep. She had checked on him before they sat down on the couch and he had cuddled his teddy bear to him, while Venture lay on the foot of the bed. Both fast asleep. Now she had not only lost Momma, but Jake too she thought, as she quietly cried and fell asleep on the couch.

The next morning when Naomer took Charlie to Mrs. Mitchell's, breakfast was waiting for them of crepes with scrambled eggs and bacon. "Honey, I need to talk to you this morning," Mrs. Mitchell told Naomer. "Sit down and let's eat though before breakfast gets cold." After they were seated and Mrs. Mitchell said grace, she continued on. "I went to the doctor a few days ago and my health is getting worse. This high altitude is affecting me also."

"Oh, I'm sorry, Mrs. Mitchell, aw didn't know you were feeling poorly."

"Well dear, I'm almost eighty years old. My children have arranged for me to move in with my daughter and her family in Sacramento, so I'll be near all of them, and they will put my home up for sale."

"Oh, Charlie and I will miss you so much. Why you've become like a grandmother to Charlie and a mother to me," Naomer said as she glanced at Charlie who had a very sad look on his face and tears in his eyes.

"Who will aw stay with?" he asked so quietly that they didn't seem to hear him.

"Well, I'll miss the both of you to. I've come to love you like my own family, and I hope you both can come and see me sometime."

"Oh, we will. I'll get somebody to show me how to get to Sacramento," Naomer answered.

"I'll be able to watch Charlie the rest of the week and I hope you can find a good place for him by then."

Naomer wondered on the way to work what she would do about finding another sitter for Charlie. On her lunch time she wrote out some ads and put them on bulletin boards at the two grocery stores in town, and the hardware and feed store. She also went to the newspaper office and placed an ad in the paper. For the first time it hit her that her and Charlie were all alone. She hadn't heard from Jake since their fight the other night and now Mrs. Mitchell was leaving them. She missed her family back home so much. But Momma was gone, how could she ever go back there–Momma wouldn't be there. Tears clouded her eyes. She drove back to the restaurant parking lot, got out and ran toward the bar. She needed a drink to settle her nerves before she went back to work.

Too days later she had a telephone call at the restaurant on the ad for boarding Charlie.The lady caller said they lived six miles out of Murphys, had three children close to Charlie's age, and the school bus went by their road. Naomer made an appointment for her and Charlie to go out to their house the next evening.

This must be the house. It looks like the small older home that the Lady described, and some pine trees in the front yard," Naomer told Charlie. The evenings were getting chilly, and the fall air was crisp. The porch light went on and a thin lady with short straight hair opened the door.

"You ms Parker?" the lady asked and wiped her hands on her apron.

"Yes, Naomer is my name, and this is Charlie."

"Well come on in," she told them and sort of ignored Charlie.

"This here's my husband, Ralph, and the kids. I'm Ruth."

"Glad ta make yore acquaintance, Naomer and Charlie," Ralph said, as he glanced up at them and continued playing solitaire with the cards laid out on an old scared up coffee table. He kept his hat on and had a two day beard. The children giggled and edged closer to Charlie.

"Well, ya all look like a cozy family. How old are you kids?" Naomer asked. "Charlie here's seven now and in the third grade."

The children didn't answer, and Ruth said, "Sara here is seven too, and Jimmy's eight and the baby's four. Her name is Carrie."

"Do ya all like school and like to ride the bus?" Naomer prompted them to talk.

"Yeah," the two older ones said. "Carrie don't go to school yet. But the bus is okay. Some times it smells like gas," Sara answered.

"Charlie always walked to school, but aw think he would like to ride the bus."

The children didn't look to well kept. Jimmy had a hole in the right knee of his jeans where his whole knee was exposed, and Carrie had a pocket partly torn off the front of her dress. Their hair was also kind of stringy like it had not been washed or brushed for days and Carrie's face was dirty.

"Why don't ja kids take Charlie and show him your bedrooms," Ruth said and then turned to Naomer, "Can aw git ya a cup of coffee?" she asked.

"Oh no, don't bother. I have to go to work this afternoon so we can only stay a little while," Naomer said and glanced around the room at the meager furnishings. The whole small room was in a disarray, which may be expected with three children, but it looked like it hadn't been cleaned for weeks.

"Where do ya'll work?" Ruth asked.

"At the Murphys Hotel and Restaurant. Am a waitress."

"Oh, ya must make pretty good wages and all," Ruth said, "How much do ya think you could pay us for boardin Charlie?" she asked in her southern accent, which was as southern as Naomers.

"Well, aw been a paying an elderly lady in town, Mrs. Mitchell, seventy-five cents a day. Would that be satisfactory to ya all?" Naomer asked. "I can't pay much more."

Ruth glanced at Ralph, and he glanced at her, then back to his card game, "Well, aw reckon maybe we'd do it for a dollar a day," Ralph replied not taking his eyes off the game.

I think aw could manage that," Naomer answered, "If we go ahead and you keep him. Am waiting for another lady in town to give me her answer as to whether or not she'll be able to keep him. She would be closer to me is all." She lied to them because she had not made up her mind yet if this would be a very good place to leave Charlie. "But as soon as I know, aw'll let ya'll know."

On the way back to town Naomer asked Charlie if he liked the kids and what he thought about staying there. "Aw liked the boy, Jimmy. Aw guess the girls are okay too," he answered.

"What did ya think about their bedrooms?" she asked.

"They were kinda plain;. I didn't see hardly any toys around."

"Were they clean? Did the bedding look clean?"

"Aw guess so. They just looked like beds, Momma. Jimmy had bunk beds. Said if I stay there aw had to sleep on the bottom."

Naomer and Charlie were still trying to remember the correct English language and still couldn't remember to say I instead of aw.

"Well, I don't rightly know if aw want you a staying there or not," Naomer went on. "They just don't seem like the right kind of folks I want you to stay with. Let's wait and see if we get more calls on the ads."

A week passed and no more calls came in for boarding Charlie. Ruth called Naomer to see if she was going to let Charlie board with them. Naomer had a feeling this wasn't something good for Charlie, but he couldn't be left alone while she worked. She would keep looking for someone else to take care of him in the mean time, but agreed to bring him over the following Sunday night.

She also knew Venture would be very lonely with both of them gone so much, but didn't think it was a good idea to inquire about Venture staying there too. She had her dog house and fenced in yard thanks to Jake, and the weather was still warm. Naomer put food and water out for her before she went to work everyday, and she had her balls, old shoes and a rubber intertube to play with.

Naomer felt more relieved Sunday night when she took Charlie to the Canon's home, as the home looked much cleaner than before, and the children were all bathed and in clean pajamas ready for bed.

Ruth woke the children up at seven o'clock the next morning to dress, eat, and catch the bus in front of the house at eight o'clock. Charlie hadn't slept too well in a strange bed, but woke up when Ruth called, and dressed in the shirt and pants his mother had arranged on top in his suitcase.

The children had oatmeal and toast for breakfast. Ruth put just a little sugar and very little milk in their oatmeal. Charlie was hungry though and ate it even though it was kind of tasteless.

"Momma, can we have some jelly for our toast?" Jimmy asked.

"There ain't no jelly," Ruth answered, "now shut up and eat so's ya don't miss that school bus."

Ralph walked into the kitchen announcing he better cut some fire wood today to burn in the stove. "Winters gonna be here afore we know it," he said. "Honey, fix me some bacon and eggs cause aw got a full days work ahead of me aw reckon,"

Ruth didn't answer, but got some bacon and eggs out of the icebox and started to cook it.

"Charlie, ya and your momma don't talk like ya'll from California, where ya from?" Ralph asked.

"We come from Alabama, sir, with Lillian and Bill on the train. We lived in Oakland for awhile, before we moved here to the mountains."

"Oh, whose Lillian and Bill?" he asked, rubbing the stubby whiskers on his face.

"Aw think Lillian is my Momma's cousin and Bill's her husband. They had a new baby this year. Where you'll from?" Charlie now returned the question.

"Oh," Ralph slowly said , "We come here from Arkansas a couple years ago. Thought we could get better wages here and more work, but can't seem to find nothin permanent. Just do odd jobs when aw can find them."

"Ya kids better hurry out that door now and catch that bus," Ruth told the kids in her loud screeching voice. "Here's ya lunch sacks, and ya lunch pail, Charlie."

"Oh, Momma, can we get lunch pails like Charlies."

"Maybe someday, now hurry on."

Charlie didn't get to see his mother for a whole week until her two days off. The Canons didn't have a telephone, so she couldn't check on him until she went to pick him up. They drove away from Charlie's new boarding place with the children standing out in the front yard waving goodbye.

"Now tell mother, how did things go this week?"

"Aw really like the kids, Momma, cept Carrie wants me to play with her all time and gets in the way."

"Well, Hon, she's just a little girl and she looks neglected. She just wants to be loved and wanted," Naomer softly said. "What about Ruth and Ralph. How did they treat ya?"

"Well," Charlie thought for a moment, "They're alright. cept they kinda talk mean to their kids. Tell um to shut up all time, and ta git out of the house and go play. Things like that."

"But they're nice to you?" Naomer asked.

"They don't talk to me much, just when they want to," he answered.

"Well, am a gonna keep looking for another place for ya. Just you try to make the best of it for now, son."

"Now what do ya want to do tomorrow? I have to clean the house in the morning, but after I'm finished we can do whatever you want."

"Aw think I just want to stay home and play with Venture."

"She really misses you. She stays in with me when I'm home, but she keeps going through the house looking for you, and a smelling your things.

"Um—she likes me, Momma."

"After I finish the house cleaning, we'll take a walk with Venture. Maybe we'll walk up town and get us all a ice cream cone," Naomer said with excitement in her voice, wanting to make it a fun thing for Charlie.

"There's a good band playing in the bar tonight, Naomer, I'm going there after I finish work, want to come along?" Karen asked.

"Sounds like fun. Sure I'll meet you there." There was usually a few cowboys and business men in the bar most of the time. Some were local residents and others passing through on business.

"You haven't heard from Jake for awhile, have you?" Karen asked, while they sit at the bar sipping their drinks.

"No. He's mad at me because aw won't marry him," Naomer answered while twisting a lock of her dark shoulder length hair around her finger. "But am a having too much fun now to git married and aw, I mean I, kinda like this freedom and independence. Jake is a real nice feller and I love him as a special friend, but aw don't think I love him enough to marry him, and be committed to someone for the rest of my life," she continued.

"Besides that, he's gone to much across country on that truck. Why that wouldn't make for a good marriage," Karen added, as she lit up a cigarette and turned her head away from Naomer to exhale the smoke. "Cigarette?" she offered one to Naomer, and lit it for her as Naomer coughed at the first inhale.

"Aw haven't smoked in front of my little boy yet. Back home it wasn't lady like for a women to smoke, but yet they chewed snuff, I never could understand that. I never did any of that, cept one time my brother swiped one of my pa's homemade roll your own, and us kids snuck outside behind the barn and smoked it. Almost made us all sick," Naomer confided, as she studied Karen's round face and wide set blue eyes. Her light creamy complection and short blond curls were something Naomer envied, even though Naomer was much prettier than her.

Just then two men, Joe and Pete, that were acquaintances of both of the women, came in and wanted to buy them a drink. They drank and danced in the dimly lit bar for several hours before Naomer realized the new drink the tried was making her dizzy and sick. She ran to the bathroom, feeling better after she returned. She knew she should quit drinking and go home but she was having too much fun, until someone said they were sorry to hear about her mother. This depressed her along with the liquor and she started crying.

"Aw wish aw could see my Ma. Aw miss her so much. Wish aw could go back home and she would be there waiting for me. Joe, order me another drink please," she mumbled on.

"Sure Babe, coming up."

Naomer was having a hard time staying on the stool. Joe kept straighting her up and holding on to her while she sat on the stool next to him. "Ya want to go home Babe, I'll take you home," he asked her several times, but Naomer just ignored him, as she studied his image in the mirror behind the bar.

She felt someone behind her touching her arm and saw Jake's image as well in the mirror. "Jake hi, what are ya a doing here?" she asked, while lifting her drink to her lips.

"I'm gonna take you home," he answered and took her arm to take her off the bar stool.

"Hey, wait a minute, Bud, who are you?" asked Joe.

"He's her boyfriend," Karen told Joe, "Now leave them alone. Naomer, you go home with Jake. You've had enough to drink tonight. She's missing her mother again, Jake."

Jake made a pot of coffee as soon as they arrived home while Naomer was sick in the bathroom. He started a fire in the fireplace and helped her out of her clothes and into some pajamas. They threw some large pillows in front of the fireplace and snuggled close together to get warm.

"Why does your Momma always make us go outside everyday?" Charlie asked Jimmy who was playing with a toy truck Charlie had brought from home.

"Aw don't know." answered Jimmy.

"It's gettin cold out here," Sara complained. "Are ya cold, Carrie?" She asked, hugging her baby sister to her.

"Me cold," answered Carrie, who was bundled up in an old snow suit that was starting to wear thin from too many washings. "Me want to go back in house," she continued.

"No. We can't yet. Moma and daddy are a probably fightin. They locked us all out," Sara told her.

It was real quiet in the house until they heard a loud bang which sounded like one of them threw something. "Ya bitch," they heard Ralph holler, "Can't ya do nothin right."

"No Ralph, please don't break the chair. We need that there chair. Aw try to do things right for you. Ralph, please don't hit me again," they heard Ruth holler and break into sobs.

"Shouldn't we do something to stop your pa?" Charlie asked, as he looked at the frightened faces of the siblings. Carrie started crying.

"If we all try to do anything, they just beat us," Jimmy said. "One time when we lived in town, Sara and me, we went to our neighbor's house, and told them our Pa was beating our mother and the neighbor came over. But after the neighbor left, our mother and dad whipped us real hard with a leather strap for telling."

"But don't ya'll love your mother?" Charlie asked with concern.

"Yeah! But aw don't think she loves us any," Sara answered thoughtfully.

"Me hungry," cried Carrie, "Me want somepin to eat."

"Well, we can't get in the house, Carrie. They have the doors locked," Sara told her again, and dug into her pocket pulling out a dried biscuit.

It was still soft enough to break and Sara broke it in half, giving Carrie half, then dividing the other half into three pieces. She handed Charlie and Jimmy both a piece and ate the last piece herself.

"We've hardly had a thing to eat all week!" exclaimed Jimmy. "They must not have any money to buy food with."

"Well, if my Mom would get here, I'd have her to go git ya'll some food," Charlie said, feeling sorry for them. "But there's no way to call her without a telephone,"

The family lived on biscuits and rice without milk or sugar, that week. Charlie sure was getting hungry for something better, and anxiously waited for his mother to come and get him on her two days off, but she didn't show up. Another week started, and the family still didn't have hardly anything to eat. Ralph left everyday saying he was looking for work, but came home in the evenings saying he couldn't find any. One day he said he chopped wood for an elderly couple and brought home a five pound sack of potatoes, some cornmeal, salt pork and milk.

Another week passed and still Naomer didn't come for Charlie. He was worried, but didn't know what to do. Ruth told him she probably just got busy at the restaurant and couldn't get any days off. Ralph and Ruth continued fighting a lot and locked the children outside when they got home from school. It was late fall and the days were getting colder and shorter. Carrie cried from being cold and the children huddled together on the porch against the house to keep warm and made up stories to tell each other for entertainment.

One day Ralph came home with a deer he had shot. The children were excited as he tied a rope to a tree in the back yard, than driving his old pickup under the tree, he tied the deer to the rope and hoisted it off the ground. He had already bled and gutted it in the forest, so now he skinned it and cleaned it with fresh water before he cut off a big chunk and carried it into the house for them to cook and eat. He moved the deer to the eve of the house and tied it there putting an old sheet around it to keep any animals away. It would hang there in the cold weather and he would continue cutting off chunks of the deer as they needed it.

Charlie liked the taste of the wild deer meat. His pants were getting so loose on him that he could hardly keep them up. He had tighten his belt as far as the notches would go. He was also getting taller and his pants looked to short for him now. The other children were always thin and looked under nourished. They had bad colds already, including Charlie, and the winter was just beginning.

He was more worried than ever about his mother. She had not been back to get him yet and almost three weeks passed without a word from her. When she finally did come for him, she apologized to him and the Canons, and said she had to work straight through because of the approaching thanksgiving holiday a lot of dinner meetings had been scheduled by groups and organizations. She felt guilty because she had been staying in the bar a lot after work and she knew she was drinking too much.

On the way home Charlie told his mother that they were almost starving until Ralph shot a deer for them to eat. "They make us stay outside a lot too, Momma, and it's cold out there. Carrie cries a lot."

"Well, I found another home for you at the edge of Murphys," Naomer told him. "It's a boarding place for boys. The people have two sons of their own, and board as many as five boys. We'll go meet them tomorrow. I talked ta the lady, Mrs. Tone, on the phone and she seems real nice."

"But what about Jimmy and Sara and Carrie, Momma, they have ta stay there," Charlie forlornly told her. "And they told me their mom and dad beats them sometimes, and aw heard Ralph cussing and beating on Ruth, Momma, several times lately."

"I don't rightly know what could be done. Those kids belong to Ruth and Ralph and the authorities just don't get involved in family situations. Aw spose I could tell Dr. Lourin and see what he said about it. Don't seem like no man should be able to go around beating his kids and wife. But then I do suppose those kids would rather stay with their real momma and daddy then to go to an orphanage home," she told Charlie.

"I don't think they would like to go there," was Charlie's response.

Naomer stopped the car in front of a huge old house with a large yard surrounding it. "I think this is the Tone Ranch," she said, smiling at Charlie, "My lands it's a lovely old place, isn't it, Charlie?"

He glanced around at the big two story white home and the yard with orchards on both sides. The fall colors vibrantly lit up the walnut and apple trees everywhere. Bright orange pumpkins lay all over in a near by garden. Charlie looked at his pretty young mother, he was a little frightened at meeting another new family. Naomer could tell he was scared and squeezed his hand. "It's going to be okay. Aw think you'll like it here."

Before Charlie opened the car door, he looked in the car mirror to see if his freckled face was clean. He pushed back a red curl that hung down on his forehead than climbed out ready to face his new family. A short heavy set lady opened the door. "Well hello, you must be Charlie," she said in a friendly manner. "Come in, Come in, Mrs. Parker."

In the living room a man was sitting in a big overstuffed chair reading a newspaper, his long legs stretched out on a hassock. He laid the paper down and got to his feet as they entered the room.

"Jack, this is Charlie our new boy, and his mother, Mrs. Parker."

"Mrs. Parker, glad to meet you," Jack said, as he shook Naomer's hand. Then looking at Charlie he held his hand out to shake his small one. "Welcome to our home, Charlie."

A thrill went through Charlie as he lifted his hand and shook the man's. "Thank ya, sir," he answered with still a hint of his southern accent. This was the first time a man had ever shook hands with him. He straightened his shoulders and stood tall and proud. He liked Mr. And Mrs. Tone right away, and hoped they felt the same about him.

The Tones told them about their own sons and the other three boys that were boarded there now, while they enjoyed fresh baked sugar cookies with milk.

"Our old dog just died, so we're looking for a young dog to take his place," Mr. Tone told them.

"Aw have a dog, a big black dog with mahogany markings. She's a rare breed called a Rottweiler," Charlie excitedly told them.

Mr. Tone took his pipe out of his mouth, "Hum–I don't think I ever heard of that breed," he said, and put the pipe back in his mouth.

"She a great dog. Real intelligent, ain't she, Momma," Charlie quickly said. "They come from Germany, and haven't been in the states very many years."

"A good friend of ours who's a long line trucker, brought the dog to us from New York," explained Naomer.

"Do ya spose we could keep her here and all the boys could play with her. Aw miss her so much when I'm gone from home," Charlie said.

"Well, what da ya think, Martha? Do you want a dog with this boy?" Jack laugh.

"Sure, why not. A boy and his dog should be together. But Charlie," She sternly said, "You'll have to share her with the other boys and not be jealous of her."

"Oh, I promise I won't be."

The next day Naomer brought Charlie, his clothes and toys and Venture back to the Tone Ranch. She didn't have long to stay and was going directly to work. Charlie took his things to his new room which he would be sharing with two of the other boys. Mrs. Tone showed him where to hang his clothes and the two drawers of the dresser which would be his. Than they got the dog dish out for Venture and filled it with fresh water, placing it in a small room off the kitchen. Venture would be able to stay in the house with them, and Mrs. Tone even put an old rug down by Charlie's bed for her to sleep on.

"Thank you, Mrs. Tone, for letting Venture come to live here too, and for lettin her stay in the house," Charlie told her.

"She's a nice dog, Charlie. I'm sure we'll enjoy the both of you staying here," she answered.

That afternoon Charlie met the other boys when they came in from school. The two older boys were the Tone's sons, Don was fifteen and Larry was thirteen. Richard, who was twelve, boarded there and had red hair like Charlies. Davy and Derald were nine year old twins.

"Well, this is all our family, Charlie," Mr. Tone told him. "Boys, I want you to meet Charlie our new boarder, and his dog Venture, whose going to be staying here also."

The boys greeted him and patted Venture, and he knew this was going to be a great place to live. After all the boys helped with the chores of feeding the three horses, thirty sheep, six pigs and four hogs, and Mr. Tone and Don milked the two cows, they sat down to supper of beans with ham hocks, cornbread, milk and apple pie for dessert. Charlie ate like he hadn't had a decent meal for a long time, and there was plenty of leftovers for Venture. Charlie remarked that Venture would get fat if she ate like that all time. Mrs. Tone laugh and said Venture looked kind of thin anyway.

"We'll fatten her up some, and what she doesn't eat it goes into the pig feed."

The boys all took turns helping Mrs. Tone with the dishes at night. Two helped each night and afterwards if there was no homework to do they all sat around the fireplace in the den. Charlie was amazed with the deer and bear heads displayed about the walls, and the boys and Mr. Tone told him how each one was shot and patiently answered his questions about the hunt. Charlie wished that he had a true exciting story like theirs to tell them. Then he thought about Jake who had promised to take him deer hunting, but never seemed to have enough time off his truck to go. Charlie became more and more excited about the adventures they told him, and he started telling them how his friend Jake had taken him deer hunting.

"We met a bear and Jake got scared and dropped his gun and ran, so aw picked the gun up and pointed it at the bear. The bear came closer and raised up on it's hind legs, striking at me with his front paws. When he was four feet from me aw shot him in the heart," Charlie told them, amazed at how fascinating he made his story sound.

He looked around the room at all of them as they were eyeing him very peculiarly with a solemn look on each face. "Charlie, we don't permit lying around here," Mrs. Tone said in her rigid manner. "You are lying, aren't you?" she asked, not so much as a question, but as a way of telling him to admit it.

"Yes, Mame," Charlie answered and hung his head. "Aw guess Aw got carried away, Mame, with the excitement and made that up. Am sorry."

Mrs. Tone brought out a wide leather strap that looked pretty worn out. She always did the spanking Charlie later found out. "Charlie, when any of the boys lie or do something terribly wrong, this belt is used to punish them. You get so many wacks according to what you do wrong. I won't use it on you this time because you're new here, but in the future you'll be punished for lying. As far as your story," she said, "you'll have a lot of adventures to tell about in your lifetime."

The Tones were strict, but they were a very close family and treated the boys that boarded there as their own sons. What the boys hated most was taking the Cod Liver Oil everyday that Mrs. Tone insisted everyone had to take to ward off colds, flu or any other sickness that may come along. It did seem to keep them all healthy, because they were hardly ever sick. Charlie felt he was loved and wanted there. He didn't get to see his mother very much through the holidays, because she was working seven days a week for awhile. But there was plenty of activities and chores to keep him occupied, and he also had to brush Venture everyday so that she could stay in the house. Venture loved it there also, and played with all the boys, but she knew she belonged to Charlie.

The boys went to a little country grammar school with only one large room and one teacher for the whole school. Charlie didn't care much for school, except for recess, and during school hours he spent a lot of time day dreaming at his desk about the exciting adventures he would have someday. Some of the kids teased him about his southern accent, which he still had most of, but he kept trying harder than ever to remember to speak the correct English. Sometimes he would lash out at the boys to shut up or even start a fist fight, which got him in trouble with the teacher, Mr. Bennette. Richard, Davy and Derald always stood up for Charlie, so sometimes all the boys in the class would start fighting.

There were four Indian children that lived about a mile from the Tone Ranch. The oldest one, Luke, was about ten years old. He was heavy set and large for his age, and bullied all the smaller boys at school. He didn't like Charlie because he could play baseball and other sports better than he could. Luke started beating Charlie up several times a week on the way home from school. Charlie had started growing and was tall for a seven year old, as tall as the nine year old twins, and excelled in sports for his young age, but Luke hovered over all of them. Richard was in an upper grade, so he got out two hours later than Charlie and the twins.

Luke tripped Charlie on the way home one day. "Huh! Can't even walk straight," Luke said, trying to provoke a fight. He continued teasing as he kicked Charlie in the stomach while he was still on the ground.

"Hey, leave him alone," Davey said and pushed Luke back, "You're always pickin on Charlie."

"Yeah, go pick on someone your own size, Luke," Derald told him.

"Come on, Luke, let's go on home and leave them alone," Luke's younger sister told him.

"Aw, shut up, all of ya," Luke hollered and kicked Charlie again.

Just as Derald and Davey were both about to jump on Luke, Charlie got up and hit Luke in the face with his Hopalong Cassity lunch pail. Luke's nose started bleeding. He cupped his hand over his nose and started running towards home, with his three siblings running after him.

When Charlie and the twins got home, Mrs. Tone was waiting for them with the leather strap. "That Indian boy came by and said you had called him names, Charlie, and hit him in the face breaking his nose with your lunch pail. My goodness he was bleeding all over," Mrs. Tone said all in one breath.

"Mrs. Tone, Luke started it," Davey said, "he's always pickin on Charlie because Charlie talks southern and Charlie can play sports better than he can."

"Yeah, he tripped Charlie and kicked him twice in the stomach before Charlie hit him with the lunch pail," confirmed Derald.

"He picks on us everyday on the way home from school, especially me," added Charlie.

"Well, why didn't you boys tell me and we would have put a stop to this someway. I'm sorry about this, Charlie," she said as she put her arm around him pulling him close, "But after this you boys tell me what's going on, and I'll talk to Mr. Bennette."

Luke left them alone after that incident, and he and his siblings hurried on towards home leaving Charlie and the twins with the pleasant adventure of finding rocks and Indian arrow heads, and talking about their dreams of growing up on the way home.

The glistening white snow covered the mountains that winter and the boys had snowball fights and built snowmen around their yard. A family Christmas was held in the large den by the fireplace, and a beautiful tall decorated Christmas tree was the center of attraction. Mr. Tone and the boys cut it on their land and the horse pulled it home. Everyone got involved with decorating it with popcorn, cranberries and decorations that had been in the Tone family for years. The boys opened their presents early that Christmas morning and Naomer and the twin's parents came for a turkey dinner that afternoon. Richard's parents were in Europe on business and had sent him a box of gifts, but couldn't come.

Charlie's thoughts often turned to Jimmy, Sara and Carrie. His mother had told him that she spoke to the doctor and a sheriff that came into the restaurant to eat a lot, but they both had said no one wanted to get involved in a family situation, because nothing would be done about it.

Jack Tone and the boys were excited about the "Frog Jump" coming up in May at Angels Camp, and started looking for a suitable frog to put in the jumping contest, and Charlie wanted to know what all the excitement was about. "What is the Frog Jump?" He asked.

"Well, Charlie," Jack started to explain, "back in 1928, a little over ten years ago, the streets in Angels Camp were finally paved and the citizens there decided to celebrate the event with a "Jumping Frog Jubilee." The frog part comes from a famous writer, Mark Twain, who spent time there in the 1860's. He had heard a tale from a bar tender there, Ross Coon, about a jumping frog, and so a contest is held for the frog that can jump the greatest distance every May."

"Sure sounds like fun. That's why we're gonna find a good frog, right?" Charlie added.

"Yes, it kind of brings back the excitement of the Gold Rush days too. The streets are filled with people and all the going ons," Jack slowly said, as though he was reminiscing about past Frog Jumps.

The hunt was on in the creek that ran through the Tone Ranch for a good jumping frog. Several frogs were tried out before one was found that could jump the farthest. He was the largest in the whole creek that they could find and decided to name him "Tone's Ole Twain." They practiced jumping him for a week before the Frog Jump. Don was to be the handler since he was the oldest.

Everyone was excited the day of the big event. They arrived there in the Tone's pickup, with all the boys and the frog in his cage, sitting in the truck bed. Charlie and the younger boys were told to stay together and had been given fifty cents each to spend. They were amazed at the carnival rides, and the large crowd of people that had come from all over the country.

Charlie bent his neck looking up at the big Ferris wheel as it went around. It looked like fun but it also looked dangerous, and he wondered how in the world did the people keep from falling off. The Ferris wheel intrigued all the boys, as well as the merry-go-round, but they decided the galloping horses was first choice and paid a nickle before they picked out one to ride on.

A proud feeling swept through Charlie and he felt important as the merry-go-round started and the horse moved up and down with it's ears back and head held high like it was going into battle. The music played loud, drowning out the other carnival noises and Charlie dreamed of riding into war with the cannons loud boom boom.

When the ride was over Charlie quietly slid off the horse, patting it's neck as though it were real. His young buddies were waiting and they continued walking around in awe of everything. They threw base balls at some objects which looked like glass milk bottles, but they were heavier and didn't break. They all won a pin wheel knocking the bottles over before they went on to another game.

The loud speaker caught their attention announcing the Frog Jump was to the north side of park.The boys squeezed between the spectators to the front, closer to the frogs and the handlers. One by one the frog's name and their handlers were announced. The crowd hollered and applauded as the frogs of their choice came up to jump. Two men with tape measures measured the jumping distant of each frog.

"Tone's Ole Twain" was the last to jump. Charlie and the boys hooped and hollered along with the crowd.

"Come on 'Ole Twain' you can jump the farthest ," they yelled. Maybe that gave 'Ole Twain' the urge he needed, because he jumped two feet further than any of the other frogs there. The crowd roared with excitement and hollered, 'Ole Twain' did it, 'Ole Twain' did it." Charlie was elated, but he wished his mother could be here to share this great event with him and the others.

Summer at the ranch was the most exciting time of year. The boys swam and fished in the creek by the ranch, and the family had picnics and barbecues. There were new boys coming to board through the year. Davey and Derald had to move with their parents to Oregon. Charlie sure missed them, but soon made friends with the new boys. They all had chores of caring and feeding all the animals and weeding the huge garden. The older boys helped irrigate the orchards and everyone helped pick the apples and walnuts in the fall. On Sundays everyone piled into the old pickup and went into town to church. Charlie received his first Bible, a white one, for attending church every Sunday for a year.

One particular day when the family was all gathered in the yard after a barbeque, it was just turning dusk and someone bet one of the older boys he wouldn't go to the cabin about a quarter of a mile from the house in the dark. The older boys didn't seem very interested in a quarter bet, but a quarter to Charlie was quite a bit, so he volunteered to do it. To show that he had been there he was suppose to bring back a small iron lid from the old stove in the cabin. The boys decided that Venture couldn't go with him for protection, so they tied her to a tree.

Charlie was scared as he walked along the dark path lined with Pine trees and Manzanita bushes. He ran aways and walked aways, imagining all kind of animal sounds he heard in the forest. An owl hooted off in the background, but it seemed to Charlie like wolves, bears and mountain lions were behind every tree. He was determined not to turn around though and be teased by the boys for months, he had to show them he was not a coward.

When he reached the cabin he opened the door and walked slowly inside. He jumped as he heard a noise in the open cupboard over head. A squirrel jumped out just missing his head and took off out the opened cabin door. An owl hooted at him before flying out a broken window. Charlie grabbed one of the lids on the stove and ran back towards the house. About half way back home he heard a noise in the trees long side the path. Whatever it was it seemed to be following him. Charlie thought again of all kinds of wild animals and even ghosts, not that he really believed in ghosts. He ran aways and than stopped to see if the noise was still following him. He saw a bush move and heard a panting sound. He was really scared than and looked at the lid he held in his hand. He threw it at the noise and let out running, but stopped when he heard a moan and someone called "Charlie wait." Don and Larry Tone stepped out into the path in the moonlight.

Larry was holding his foot moaning again, and Charlie thought to himself, 'oh aw really had it now.'

"It's okay, Charlie, It's our fault for scaring ya. We just followed you to protect you, but we thought it might be fun to kind of scare ya a little," Don laugh.

When they got back to the yard and told everyone what happened and showed them the stove lid, Mr. Tone gave Charlie the quarter. They checked Larry's foot and it was bruised but not broken. For a few days Charlie was treated like a King and the other boys even did his chores, but he got kind of tired of it and everything went back to normal.

Charlie lived at the Tone Ranch for a year and a half. His last day there was very sad. Leaving the Tones was like leaving grandparents again and the boys were all like his brothers. Naomer had decided to take a job at a busy establishment in Wallace, called Rosetties. It was an Italian restaurant and bar ran by Italian immigrants, and known for having the best Italian food for miles around. Naomer and Charlie would live with the Rosetties above the restaurant and huge dance hall.

When Naomer arrived for Charlie at the Tone Ranch, he was sitting with Venture in the drying shed, eating Black Walnuts and sulking about leaving along with day dreaming about what his next home would be like. This was his favorite hideaway when he wanted to be alone and think. He had his suit cases packed and was ready to go. Reluctantly he said his goodbys to everyone and watched with tears in his eyes as everyone stood in the front yard waving as they drove away.

Jake had become tired of waiting for Naomer and had came over and told her he was going to marry a young lady from Sonora he had been seeing. Naomer wished him well, but felt lonely and sad for several weeks because he would no longer be her best friend, the only one she really had to depend on and talk to about problems with Charlie or anything else.

Lillian and Bill had went back to Alabama for a visit and to show off their new son and had decided to stay there. Bill had obtained a good job in construction there, since he had learned a lot about construction on the San Francisco jobs. Naomer didn't get to see them very much after she moved to the mountains, but she always knew they were close if she really needed them or could always call them on the telephone.

The news of the World War II war was the main topic on the radios all over United States. The war was scary in the big cities of Oakland and San Francisco, as talk of the Atomic bomb was becoming more real, and the larger cities would be bombed first if it happened. Franklin D. Roosevelt had been re-elected president on November 5, 1940, and the U. S. Had their factories in full swing making guns, ammunition, tanks, planes and ships by 1941.

It was a scary time for everyone, but yet in a small town like Wallace, California, a young boy didn't yet feel the affects of the war. The Rosetties were a close family. Papa Rosettie's wife had died several years earlier, so he cared for his two young daughters, about eleven and seven years old. An older son lived in San Francisco, but came home to Wallace often.

Summer was fun that year for Charlie after all. He got to see his mother all time, and the Rosettie girls were a lot of fun. They played games through the week in the big dirt parking lot of the restaurant, such as 'Kick the Can' and 'Anny, Anny over.' Venture loved these games and joined in with them, sometimes running off with the can or ball.

On Friday and Saturday nights huge crowds would come there to eat, drink and dance. Charlie and the girls were sent off to bed upstairs, but they would climb on top of their dressers looking over a wall to watch the crowd below on the dance floor. This probably wasn't in their best interest, because they saw about everything on that dance floor, but if they were quiet no one would suspect they did this.

"Orson and Logan Lamb" and "The Happy Hay seeds", played with their bands there most of the time. Once in awhile "Daddy Zarko and his Ozark Mountaineers" would play. Charlie loved to hear Daddy Zarko's daughter, Luella Gosnell, sing "I'm a Cowboy's Sweetheart." She had a voice like an angel and Charlie was mesmerized every time she sang.

One sunny morning Charlie and Janet, the youngest Rosettie daughter, decided to pack a lunch and hike about a half mile to the reservoir. They were going through the restaurant kitchen looking for something to take along that Papa or the cook had made. Charlie liked the taste of Italian food, but most of it was so rich for him until he got use to it, that it made him sick.

They walked through a wooded area and a pasture to get to the reservoir. Venture stayed right in front of them on the trail as though she had to protect them. The sun was straight up in the sky and the summer day was starting to get hot.

"Am a gettin kind of hungry!" Charlie exclaimed.

"Me too a little," Janet answered. "Let's put our blanket here and unload this basket we been carrying. It's getting heavy." She took out salami and pepperoni and several different kinds of sliced cheese. "Oh here's some Proscuitto," Janet announced.

"What is it," asked Charlie, as he took a piece.

"It's ham, silly," Janet said, "and look we have some pickled artichoke hearts and celery stuffed with anchovy cream cheese."

"How do you know what all this stuff is?" asked Charlie.

"Cause I help sometimes in the kitchen," she answered.

"Bet the people that come there to eat get sick a lot than," Charlie teased.

"Oh be quiet," Janet said, hitting him on the arm.

Charlie unwrapped two large barbequed rib bones with some meat on them they had brought for Venture, and put them down about five feet from their picnic food. "Now stay here Venture and eat these," he ordered her.

They were quiet for awhile while they enjoyed their food. A large orange-black Monarch butterfly landed next to their blanket. "Be still and let's see what this butterfly is going to do," Janet said.

"Want me to catch him for you?" asked Charlie.

"No, Charlie, I want that butterfly to be free. God made it and set it free. My mother said we should never catch butterflies or birds. They need to fly and be free spirits. The butterfly flew off and their attention turned to other talk.

"I'll be glad when school starts. Do you like school," She asked."

"A little bit, but not a whole lot. I like recess and baseball and football. That sure is a little school house where we'll be going next to the restaurant," Charlie said.

"Well it holds all the kids. There ain't very many kids around Wallace. They're all together in that one room from first through eighth grade," Janet told him.

"Aw went to a great big school in Oakland. It had eight rooms, one for each grade and a big cafeteria and a big auditorium for Christmas plays and music and stuff," he told her, as he ate the last piece of stuffed celery.

"I don't think I would like a great big school. Oh, that suns hot," Janet said wiping her face with a wet napkin they had brought along. "Come on, let's pick up our picnic stuff and I'll show you the water and the rock slide."

They walked another quarter of a mile to the reservoir. Charlie said it was pretty there, but not as pretty as the little creek that ran behind the Tones home. He missed the Tones and the beauty of their orchards and hills and forests.

"See Charlie, there's the rock slide going down that bank." Charlie looked. There was a small amount of water running down the smooth rocks, just enough to make them slippery. The kids stripped to their bathing suits and ran toward the slide.

"Let me go first, Charlie, you come behind me," Janet told him as she sat on the first rock and pushed off to slip down followed by Charlie. The slide was about twenty feet to the bottom and Janet stirred up a rattle snake sunning himself on a rock on the slide. She went right over him and he started to slitter away when Charlie slid into him knocking him down the rocks ahead. Janet moved out of the way and the snake was trying to slitter away, but when Charlie landed next to him he started coiling. Fear gripped Charlie as he stared at the coiled snake not more than two feet from him. Janet too seemed paralyzed staring at the snake. In the mean time Venture's animal instinct had told her the kids were in some kind of danger sliding down that rock slide, and had made her way to the bottom of the slide by going down the bank farther up the path and back tracking. When Venture saw the snake almost ready to strike at Charlie she darted in grabbing it behind it's head and shaking it, giving Charlie a chance to move away, before she flung it away from them. The wounded snake was all to happy to crawl away from the three of them.

"Boy that was a close call," Janet said, still trying to get her breath.

"Yeah, I thought he was going to strike at me. Come here Venture, good dog. You saved our lives," Charlie told her as he hugged and kissed her. Janet hugged her too, "Good girl, Venture."

The cold fall weather kept people home more on the weekends and the restaurant business was very slow. Plus a lot of the men were joining or being enlisted into the service. The war was on every ones mind and they didn't talk about much else. Naomer had been offered a job in Lockeford, a small town about twelve miles west of Wallace. It was larger than Wallace and she was offered more wages at the restaurant and bar there.

The people were friendly and everyone seemed to know each other. She had been going with a cowboy that rode the rodeo circuit, and his folks boarded several boys at a time on their ranch where they raised rodeo stock. She thought this would be good place for Charlie to get some ranch training and he loved the idea of being able to work with horses and cattle. Of course most of the stock was wild and the boys were not allowed to get around it, but there were plenty of other chores to do and a number of trained horses to ride there.

The war was still going on and Pearl Harbor was attacked by the Japanese on December 7, 1941. The whole United States was in a turmoil. Thousands of American citizens of Japanese ancestry were herded into internment camps by the government. Japanese children that went to schools were missing all of a sudden. Workers were missing. All of them were sent to the camps until the war would end. People everywhere were rationed on gasoline and food among other things. At night there were blackouts. The lights in homes had to be kept low, and dark green shades were put up on windows around America so the enemy couldn't see the lights and attack.

Charlie's new home was a long bunk house where he slept with four other boys which were all a year or two older than him. They had to keep the bunk house clean, but could do anything they wanted there without too much supervision, except when Mr. Stergeon, the owner of the ranch, inspected it once a week it had to be cleaned. They ate their meals three times a day, at six o'clock in the morning, at noon and six o'clock in the evening. The boys did chores of feeding the animals , keeping the huge barn swept and cleaned, and the stalls cleaned. Also grooming the tame animals, weeding the huge garden and doing the yard work. It seemed as though the boys would have been paid wages for all this work, but instead of paying wages the owners of the ranch called it training and charged less board money from the boy's parents.

Several of the boys had been in some trouble and instead of the judge sending them to Juvenile Hall he went along with the parent's wishes of sending them to the ranch to work. Naomer's boyfriend, Luke, failed to tell her any of this. He only told her it was a good place for a young fellow to learn how to work and learn discipline.

Charlie went with the other boys to a larger school than the little one in Wallace where he had began the school year. He was the youngest boy at the ranch with only two others, Paul and Samuel, going to grammar school. The two older boys, Harry and Bob, were in high school.

The winter was cold that year and the bunk house wasn't very warm. A large old wood stove in the middle of the building was used to heat it. It kept the boys busy chopping wood to keep the stove going. Charlie had brought several extra blankets from home to keep warmer at night, because if no one remembered to put wood in the stove through the night it was freezing cold toward morning. Venture got to go along with Charlie and slept at the foot of his twin size bed. She had to be tied up to an old oak tree next to the bunk house while Charlie attended school, and sometimes when the boys rode horses, because she seemed to think the boys were going to get hurt when they rode.

Charlie had learned to ride a horse at the Tone Ranch, but only got to ride in the pasture there. Here the five boys got to saddle each one a horse sometimes on Saturday, if they were not too busy, and ride three miles to the Mokelumne River.

Mrs. Stergeon rang the dinner bell and the boys came from the barn where they had been cleaning the stalls and sweeping the barn. Going to the wash house first to wash up, where Samuel had just brought a clean bucket of water from the well. They then filed into the large dinning room for a hot noon meal. The ranch foreman, who was just called Cowboy, also had meals with them and lived in a small one room cabin next to the bunk house. Charlie was aware that the boys didn't like Cowboy from the conversations he heard in the bunk house. They said Cowboy was mean, and too never cross him if you didn't want to be in real trouble. Mr. Stergeon was getting old and walked partially with a cane because he had arthritis in his joints. He was cranky most of the time and if something didn't go right he would cuss and holler at the boys. Mrs. Stergeon was about fifteen years younger than her husband. She was pretty in an ordinary way, maybe a bit on the plump side, but she was a good cook and kept the house somewhat clean. However, the older boys were always talking about how she hung on them a lot and had seen her a number of times sneaking into Cowboy's cabin. The two other ranch hands that took care of the rodeo stock had the noon meal at the ranch also, but went home to their families at night.

Luke was the Stergeon's only son, and was on the rodeo circuit most of the time. He had an overbearing manner Charlie thought. He was arrogant, and bragged a lot about riding wild horses and bulls to the point that Charlie didn't really see why his mother liked him. Maybe Charlie was jealous, also because if Luke was home for a weekend than Charlie had to stay at the ranch and work instead of spending the two days at home with Naomer.

An argument was pursuing between Mr. Stergeon and Cowboy at the table over feeding the rodeo stock some bad oat hay they had just purchased.

"That hay ain't fit for rodeo stock," Cowboy argued.

"Well it's what they'er a gona git. The stock don't have no work to do this winter. Come spring we'll feed some better hay," Mr. Stergeon hollered at Cowboy.

"We're gona end up with a bunch of sick animals this winter if you feed that alone," Cowboy came back.

"What do you fellers think?" Mr. Stergeon asked the other two hired hands.

"Well, aw know the better feed cost a lot more, but we think Cowboys right about not feeding that bad hay. It ain't bad aw spose, but it still ain't got no nutrients in it to amount to a hill of beans," one of the men said, while he nervously wiped his mustache with a cloth napkin.

"I've been a raising livestock for sixty years, but you knuckleheads are probably right. Alright, we'll get some good alfalfa. Mr. Stergeon told them.

Charlie breathed a sigh of relief. He was glad that argument was finished, but another one would soon start he thought, because it was this way at every meal between Mr. Stergeon and cowboy, or else one of them would start in on one of the boys. All the boys finished eating and asked to be excused to return to their work. It was Charlie's job this Saturday to straighten up the tack room and polish one of the saddles, which he was working on when Cowboy came in looking for a certain halter. He saw Venture laying next to Charlie and kicked her.

"Git out of here ya mangy dog," he hollered, and Venture yelped and ran out the door knocking over the can of oil Charlie had been using on the saddle.

"Don't kick my dog," he yelled at Cowboy.

"Well look at what she done, spilled that darn expensive oil," Cowboy said hatefully.

"Well she wouldn't of done it if ya wouldn't of kicked her," answered Charlie.

"Hey boy, ya know who you're a talking to?" he asked, as he shut the door and pulled off his belt. "You're a talking to the boss here?" he grabbed Charlie and threw him over a saddle which was sitting on a sawhorse and hit him five times on his butt and back while Venture barked at the door knowing Charlie was in trouble. Now get this oil cleaned up and don't you breath a word about me spanking ya ta anyone or I'll kill that there dog of yours, ya hear?" Cowboy opened the door, hollering at Venture to get out of the way, still slinging his belt around as he left. Charlie hugged Venture when she ran in to him, while she whimpered to console him.

Charlie kept quiet and didn't tell anyone what Cowboy had done, not even telling his mother. He had seen this happen with the other boys too and heard him threaten them. Not even Mr. Stergeon knew, but he probably wouldn't have done anything about it anyway, he was so mean too, Charlie thought to himself.

The older boys were always plotting to get even with Cowboy when they sit around the bunkhouse in the evening talking, but Charlie guessed they were afraid to go through with any of it, as all they ever did was talk.

When Charlie went home for the weekends with his mother he just stayed in the apartment where she lived in a old building above a restaurant and bar in Lockeford. He didn't know any of the boys in town since he went to a country school way out of town. Sometimes they would go to a movie theatre in Lodi, a larger town about twelve miles away.

Naomer didn't talk about Luke to much to Charlie, because she knew Charlie didn't care for him, and she was beginning to realize he wasn't the man she thought he was at first. His priorities seem to change after he thought she had fallen in love with him, and now he was starting to get bossy and possessive, something no man was ever going to do to her again.

She missed Jake a lot, but she wasn't sorry she had not married him. According to some of their old friends which Naomer occasionally saw, Jake was very happy, but had asked about her and said he missed her and Charlie.

After the first spanking from Cowboy, Charlie tried to stay out of his way as much as possible, but it seemed Cowboy always found something wrong with Charlie's work and continued spanking him with his belt in the tack room when no one else was close by. He also continued threatening him if he told, he would kill Venture. One of the older boys, Harry, heard Charlie crying one day in the tack room and questioned him.

"He spanks me every week for something. Say's I don't do my work right, but aw don't know how else he wants me ta do it," Charlie sniffled. "And he says if I tell anyone he'll kill Venture. So please don't tell Mr. and Mrs. Stergeon," begged Charlie.

"I won't tell them. But that dirty----------," Harry didn't continue the name he was thinking. "He's been pulling the same game with the rest of us too. We're gona get him someway, I promise."

Later that week the boys were left alone at the ranch on Saturday. The Stergeons went into town to get supplies and groceries, the two ranch hands had to deliver some rodeo stock out of town, and Cowboy, who should have stayed home with the boys that day, left too. Cowboy had put a young two year old gelding into the corral that he was trying to break and the boys thought it would be fun to try to ride him.

"Whose going first?" asked Bob.

"I'll take the first shot at him," Harry said, "That way he'll be wore down for you guys."

"Oh sure, ya think ya can ride him long enough to wear him down. We'll see," answered Bob.

Cowboy had already saddled the gelding and left it on him to get him used to a saddle. The young horse bucked slowly a couple of times after Harry climbed on him. He wasn't from the rodeo stock and had been handled some in his two years, so he wasn't a mean horse. He bucked slowly a few more times than just stood there like he didn't know what else to do.

"Okay whose next?" asked Harry, as he slid off the horse.

"Me, I want to ride him," Charlie quickly said.

"Are ya sure, Charlie, you're only ten, even though you got those long legs on ya," Harry asked him.

"I'm sure," he answered, putting his leg in the stirrup and swinging his other leg over the saddle.

The gelding started bucking immediately, harder bucks than when Harry was on him, but Charlie hung onto the saddle horn and the reins tightly, perhaps too tightly, because the horse went into a spin with Charlie holding on and his legs and feet tight in the stirrups.

"Hang on, Charlie, ride em Charlie," the other four boys hollered, while Charlie rode him out.

"Whee------that was a good ride," Harry said, "whose next?"

"Guess it's my turn," Bob said, climbing on the tired horse that just walked around the corral for awhile before Bob cracked him a few times with the reins which started him to bucking again.

"I think we'll have this here horse broke before Cowboy gets back," Harry laugh.

The horse was getting tired and mad with all these boys getting on him and he really started bucking hard this time. "Stay with him, Samuel," Harry hollered and looked worried as he spit out a chew of tobacco.

The horse kept bucking and Samuel couldn't stay on, falling to the ground he hit hard and lay there very still while the other four boys ran in the corral to him.

"Paul, go get some water from the well. Bob, keep the horse back away from us while I try to revive him," Harry told them while he patted Samuel on the cheeks, "Samuel wake up, wake up."

"Will he be alright, Harry," Charlie asked.

"Sure as soon as we get him to come to."

Paul ran up with a half bucket of water and Harry poured almost the whole amount on Samuel who started coming to. "Oh my leg hurts," he said and tried to reach down to his leg.

"Does it feel broken?" asked Harry.

"Yeah, I think so. Oh it hurts."

"Well, we're gona have ta get you to the hospital someway," Harry told him.

Just then Mr. and Mrs. Stergeon pulled into the driveway. They saw the boys in the corral and drove back there instead of stopping at the house.

"Just what the Sam Hells going on here?" Mr. Stergeon said as he got out of the pickup with his cane.

"we think Samuel has a broken leg," Harry told him.

"And how in the Hell did that happen?" he asked.

"Well, we were trying to break this here gelding," said Harry.

"Now you boys know you're not suppose to break any of the horses. Where's Cowboy?"

"He left shortly after you and the Mrs. did," Harry answered, hoping Cowboy would get into trouble over this too.

"Well, I'll be dang gum it, I can't trust anybody around here, now can I?" He said, as he felt Samuel's leg. "Yeah boy, I think it's broken, maybe in two places. You boys, Bob, Charlie, Paul help me unload these supplies in the pickup at the house and then I'll come back and take Samuel to the hospital, Harry, you stay here and watch him."

After Mr. Stergeon, Harry and Samuel returned from the hospital and got Samuel settled into his bed in the bunk house, Cowboy returned about dark. Mr. Stergeon was waiting for him.

"What the Sam Hell do you mean leaving these boys here alone?" He asked Cowboy.

"Aw ain't no nursemaid, I'm a ranch foreman," he came back at Mr. Stergeon.

"But I told you before when I have ta go away that you're ta watch over the boys. Now we got one with a broken leg because you had to go get your gut full of beer and chase after those little fillies at the bar. If this happens again, you're fired, ya hear, fired?' he said as he left out the door with the boys trying not to snicker in front of Cowboy. They were all very pleased to see Cowboy get in trouble, but hated to suffer the consequences of what he would probably have in store for them.

And they were right. He pushed so much work on them that spring and if it wasn't done exactly the way he wanted, he punished the boys by not letting them have privileges of riding the horses, listening to the radio, or other things he knew they liked to do. He would also spank the younger boys in the tack room when no one was around and threatened all of them if they told.

Harry and Bob, who were both sent to stay there a year by the court, talked about running away. Samuel wanted to go with them as he had no parents, only an aunt and uncle who didn't want him and sent him to the ranch so they wouldn't be burdened with him. Paul would be leaving soon as he was moving with his family to another state. And Charlie thought it might be fun to run away, but he loved his mother and knew she would be very worried about him, and he wondered how he could feed Venture being out on his own. Mr. and Mrs. Stergeon didn't care about the boys, they only wanted them there to work for free and to get board for them.

Everyone had just finished supper and went to finish up some work outside before dark. Cowboy was halter breaking a four month old colt in the corral while the dam was nervously watching from a stall close by and whinnying to her foal. The foal, wanting to go to his mother's calls, wouldn't do what Cowboy wanted, so he kicked the foal over and over and started beating him with the long lead rope. Well this was more than Harry and Charlie could take. They both ran to Cowboy and Harry hit him with his fist while Charlie grabbed the lead rope and pulled the foal away. Harry who was almost as tall and lanky as Cowboy, beat him up good, giving him a bloody nose and black eye. Harry even threatened him by telling him if he didn't start leaving all the boys alone he was going to Mr. Stergeon to tell him everything that was going on, even about seeing Mrs. Stergeon sneaking into Cowboy's cabin at different times.

Naomer was still going with Luke, but he only came home now about once a month for a few days, and she was kind of tired of this, but she was spending more time on the weekends with Charlie. They would go shopping, go to a movie and eat out quite a bit, which Charlie loved to do.

A knock at the door sent Charlie and Venture both running to unlock the apartment door. "Well hello Charlie, didn't think you'd be here already on a Friday night."

"Hi Luke," Charlie said, in a bored manner. "Mom, Lukes here."

"Oh Luke! I didn't think you'd be here this weekend," Naomer said, with no excitement in her voice.

"Well evidently not, ya already picked up Charlie, aw see," he said kind of sarcastically. Aw was gona take ya out dancing tonight. Can we take Charlie back to the ranch for the weekend?" he asked. "I won't be back for several months. Have ta go to Texas and Oklahoma for some big rodeos back there for awhile."

"Luke, I'm tired of you being gone all the time, and I'm tired of a lot of other things that you do that really aggravated me, so why don't you just go downstairs to the bar and find one of your old girlfriends. I'm sure there are plenty down there, and take them dancing," Naomer harshly told him, adding "I don't want to go with you anymore. You're just not the person I thought you were."

"Ah------, come on, sugar baby, you know aw love ya. Don't be mad at me cause aw been gone a lot," he said moving towards her.

"No, just go, Luke, I mean it. I don't want to see you again."

He reached for her, but Venture stepped in and growled showing all her canine teeth, warning him to back off. "Okay, okay, I'll leave, but you're gona be sorry, Naomer, ya let me slip through your fingers, cause I'm gona be famous and rich real soon, just wait and see," he said as he went out the door.

Charlie and Naomer started laughing until it doubled them in two, and Charlie was glad his mother had returned to her old self again, and saw Luke for what he was.

Cowboy left the boys alone more after Harry beat him up and quite beating on the animals so much also. The boys didn't talk much about running away anymore and everything settled down for awhile. Charlie also heard that Luke had got his draft papers and was being sent into the army.

Harry and Bob's year was up and they moved back home with their parents. Two new boys took their places at the ranch and the pattern seemed to start again with Cowboy bossing all of them around, threatening them, and the spankings in the tack room also resumed again.

Charlie had never told his mother about all the spankings Cowboy gave him, because he was desperately afraid Cowboy would kill Venture. He also didn't tell his mother that he had fallen back in his school grades this year because he was so tired at night from all the work he did on the ranch that he didn't feel like doing homework and besides no one was there to tell him to do it. He gave his report cards to Mrs. Stergeon who just looked at them and signed them without reading anything the teacher had written on them. Maybe she couldn't read Charlie thought. None the less if he didn't pass this school year he would have to tell his mother why.

Naomer was young and had not had much schooling herself. She had quit school and married at fifteen years old and had a baby nine months later. She couldn't read much better than Charlie could. Perhaps this was the reason for not disciplining him and molding his character when he was boarded out because she thought it should be done by older people that he stayed with. She didn't know all the rules, because she had not achieved them herself yet.

It was about this time that Naomer met a special man. Ed was different than any other man Naomer had ever known. He was quiet, yet strong, and being with him gave her a feeling of security she had never experienced before. He was short, maybe a half inch shorter than her, and stocky built of solid muscle. He was of German heritage and still lived at home with his mother and father who were well respected in the small town of Lockeford. His father was a well digger and knew everyone all over the country. He was from a large family and was the youngest, with the other siblings living in distant towns. He only had one problem, when he drank he liked to fight, and had never lost a fight yet. This only made him more desirable in Naomer's eyes.

She had invited Ed over for supper one Saturday night when Charlie was staying with her so they could meet. "You be on your best behavior tonight, and we'll try to get Ed to open up and talk more," She told Charlie.

"Why? Don't he like to talk, Mom?"

"Well, yeah, but he's kind of quiet. I think he's kind of bashful too."

Charlie opened the door and let Ed in. "You must be Charlie."

"Yep! Hi, Momma will be right out. She's still dressin'.

Venture sat down in front of Ed where he sat on the couch, and wagged her short stumpy tail looking pleadingly at him to be petted. Ed looked as thought he didn't know for sure if he should reach out to pet her, but gently laid his hand on her head and rubbed it.

"I've had several dogs through the years. I never saw one like this though," he said as he continued to rub her head.

"She's a Rottweiler. Not very many of em in United States. Momma's old boyfriend bought her for me in New York."

"Oh!" Ed exclaimed, looking kind of uneasy when Charlie mentioned an old boyfriend of Naomers.

"She's a good watch dog. She loves people, but if you came around when we weren't here she would bark and growl and show her teeth and not let you in," Charlie rambled on in his usual way when he had a listener.

Just then Naomer entered the room and Ed stood up. "Oh, don't get up. Supper is just about ready. I hope you like baked chicken and dressing."

"I like any kind of food," Ed smiled with his dark eyes shining.

Small talk was resumed through supper about the war, the well drilling business that he was in with his dad, and about their families. They all three did the dishes together and Charlie went off to bed with Venture to listen to Fibber McGee and Molly on the radio.

Naomer moved closer to Ed on the couch. She felt him tense up, but she snuggled closer. If he was ever going to kiss her she was going to have to make the first move. She laid her hand on his and surprisingly he put her hand in his, squeezing it gently.

"I've known you exactly two months," he drifted off, "and well I've never really had a girl friend I liked as much as you. Well, I was wondering if you would marry me?" he asked.

"Really, ya want ta marry me? Do you love me, Ed?"

"I wouldn't ask you to marry me if I didn't," he answered.

"Oh Ed, you're so different than anyone aw ever knew before. But I think maybe I do love you. And yes I'll marry you."

Ed awkwardly kissed her as Naomer wondered what it would be like to teach him the art of love making.

The next day Naomer excitedly told Charlie that Ed had asked her to marry him.

"He don't say much to me, Momma, I don't think he likes me."

"He's quiet I know, but I'm sure he really likes you, Charlie. He just don't know how to act around kids. And guess what? He wants me to quit working and just stay home and be a housewife and you can move back home and start school next year in Lockeford."

With only a month of school left this year Charlie studied real hard for the last test, hoping not to flunk the fifth grade. He had to let some of his work go sometimes in the evenings which made Cowboy mad, than it was back to the spanking room. One particular evening Charlie had left some of the gardening tools out in the yard and Cowboy caught him dragging him to the tack room. The other boys had already went to the bunkhouse and Venture was tied to the tree. Well Venture saw what was happening and barked loud and continuously pulling on her rope until she got loose. Cowboy had not tightly closed the door, and Venture got through the door, attacking Cowboy as he was whipping Charlie with a leather lead strap. By that time the other boys had heard all the commotion and ran outside with one of them getting Mr. Stergeon and all running to the tack room where the noise was coming from. Charlie finally call Venture off of Cowboy and calmed her down, but not before she ripped a small gash in his arm and on his face and had torn his shirt off.

"What the Sam Hells going on here now?" Mr. Stergeon asked, "What's this all about?"

"Dam dog attacked me. I'm gona git my gun and kill her," Cowboy said as he staggered to his feet.

"Now just hold on here a minute," Mr. Stergeon continued, "That dog must have had some reason to attack you. What happened, Charlie?" he asked.

Well Sir, Cowboys been a spanking all of us ever since aw came here. With a leather strap or his belt. And he said if I ever told anybody he would kill Venture."

"Is this true, boys?" Mr. Stergeon said looking at the other boys.

"Yes Sir, we all got black and blue stripes on our bodies from it." The younger boys said and took their shirts off to show him.

My God, Cowboy, you been beating these boys like this. You get your things and get out of here tonight. Don't you ever step foot back on this ranch again. And don't you come back here tonight scaring these boys, and you leave that dog alone. She had every right attacking you like she did. You do anything else here and I'll have you jailed for beatin minors. Now get out. You boys all go to the bunkhouse right now and take Venture and lock the door. I'll see to it that Cowboy leaves."

In the middle of the night Charlie woke from a deep sleep with Venture barking loudly and a voice hollering "fire, fire." He realized it was Samuel's voice and the smell of smoke curled around his nostrils causing him to cough and choke. He jumped out of bed and woke the other two boys next to him. Samuel ran to the house to get the Stergeons to call the fire department. The whole bunkhouse was destroyed by time the fire department got there. The boys had saved some of their belongings, but Mr. Stergeon wouldn't let them go back in when he got out to it. The rest of the night they all slept on pallets on the floor in the Stergeon's house.

Cowboy was never found by the sheriffs and had probably left the country after he set the fire. The boys had to go back home until a new bunkhouse was built. Charlie moved back with his mother and she drove him to school to finish the last two weeks. He passed to the next grade, but was sure his teacher felt sorry for him with the fire and all that had happened.

Naomer and Ed decided to go to Reno, Nevada the end of summer to get married, as Naomer had no family here and Ed's family did not seem too anxious for him to marry her. After all, she worked in a bar and restaurant and had a young son with no father.

Naomer's apartment was too small for the three of them, so it was decided that they could live with Ed's folks until the people could move out of Ed's small home that he rented out. It would have to be painted and fixed up some before they moved into it.

Charlie had to stay with his new grandmother, Anna, and grandfather, Godfried, while his mother and Ed went to Reno to be married and take a three day honeymoon there. It was almost like living in a foreign country when the old couple talked German to each other and Charlie had no idea what they were talking about.

They were nice to Charlie, but yet aloof. Charlie was growing taller and filling out and required a lot of food now, but Anna put meager helpings on the table and he didn't want to act like a pig. The food she prepared was almost all German cooked and Charlie's taste buds were not yet accustomed to it.

The day Naomer and Ed had planned to come home, Anna had baked four pies and sat them in the open window to cool. Now Charlie being so hungry for three days couldn't resist swiping one of these whole pies while she was over visiting at the neighbors. He grabbed a fork in the kitchen and an apple pie from the window sill and he and Venture headed for the tank house to eat it. It tasted so good they ate the whole thing and hid the pie plate and fork, while Charlie made a mental note to slip them back into the house in a day or two.

He had also noticed a plate of chicken gizzards sitting on the kitchen sink and grabbed one of them when he went back into the house, stuffing it into his mouth when he suddenly heard a door slam shut. It was only the wind that closed the door, but Charlie tried to swallow the gizzard and it stuck right in his throat. He was chocking and starting to loose his breath, but was still conscious enough to know he needed help. He ran out the front door towards the neighbors where he knew Anna was at and met her coming across the lawn when he lost conciosness and fell flat on his stomach. With that, the gizzard plopped out of his mouth bouncing down the sidewalk right up to Anna's feet. Charlie came to at about the same moment. Looking up at Anna Sheepishly, he grinned.

"Jou bad boy," she said in her a broken English. "Jou got into mine gizzards. Shame on you."

"Am sorry, Grandma Anna. I was hungry," he answered.

"Well, jou don't ever do dat again. Understand? And joust call me Anna."

Anna never said anything about one of her pies missing. But Charlie stayed out of her way for three or four hours that day. Anna also never told anything about the gizzard incident to Naomer. Charlie didn't know if she had forgotten it or if she didn't want to get him in trouble with his mother, but whatever the reason he was thankful.

The Lockeford School that Charlie went to that fall consisted of three small buildings which held classes from first grade through eighth. They played more baseball and football there because there were more children. Charlie excelled in sports, but was still behind in his reading and spelling. Math and history came easy to him because he liked those subjects.

Naomer and Ed started repairing, painting and wallpapering the house, so that they could move out of his folk's home and be to themselves. Charlie wanted to help, and learned how to handle a paint brush quite well without getting to much paint on him. The house set on five acres with the back property connecting to the river bottom and the Mokelumne River.

"We got our own home now, Venture, and wait till summer we can swim in the river," Charlie told his canine companion who seemed to be almost as happy as Charlie. "We can have some chickens and ducks and rabbits and pigs and maybe our own horse even."

Naomer had quit working just before they got married and would be staying home to take care of Ed and Charlie. She decided to take in ironing to help out with expenses and to give her something to do with her extra time. At first she wasn't excepted by the other women in town, but she volunteered to help at the watch tower for sightings of enemy aircraft, and soon become friends with a lot of them. She was hoping to have a child soon and knew it was Charlie's dream to have a brother or sister.

Ed continued working with his dad in the well drilling business until he had saved up enough money to buy a milk truck with a route. The route was very early hours seven days a week, but he liked it a lot better than drilling wells, and his father was hard to get along with.

Charlie started a farm on the acreage. It already had several chicken coops on it and some rabbit pens. He was given some Muscovy and Mallard ducks, geese, Chinese Chickens and Pigeons, which all multiplied fast. He bought several rabbits and built more pens, holding at about seventy five does. He and Naomer dressed out the young rabbits and sold them to neighbors and grocery stores. He learned how to dry the skins and shipped them off to a company which paid him twenty five to thirty five cents per skin. With the money he made from the rabbits he bought an old Guernsey cow to raise drop calves on, and also a sow that would soon have a litter of pigs.

With all these animals to feed Charlie ask for a job after school at the local feed store. He was hired for two hours after school to sweep up the floors, and could take all the wasted feed he swept up home to his animals. Usually he would have a half a sack a day of barley, oats, wheat and anything else he swept up. Then he would stop in the evenings at the three local grocery stores and pick up the wasted vegetables they were throwing away. Ed brought home any rejected milk he had for the day from the route. If it didn't pass the creamery qualifications a light blue vegetable dye was put into it so that it couldn't be sent back. The grain and milk Charlie cooked together, along with some of the vegetables, in a large pot outdoors over a wood fire. For the pigs it was good and nutritious. Rabbit pellets was about the only thing he had to purchase.

One evening after Charlle had fed all his animals and came in to wash up for supper, Naomer hugged him, "Guess what, son?" she said with excitement in her voice. Than not waiting for him to answer said, "We're going to have a baby in the fall."

"A real baby?" Charlie asked, "you mean a brother or sister?"

"A real human baby," she answered smiling, hugging him again.

"Does dad know yet?"

"Not yet. I just came from the doctor's office."

Charlie felt like his life was being completed. He was settled here to stay. He had a stable home now with a dad, and the farm he always wanted, a lot of new friends, and now a brother or sister coming.

He did wish he could get closer to Ed though. He felt Ed really did care for him, but Ed didn't show a lot of emotion. Sometimes it seemed like Ed was even jealous of him and his mom. Charlie could see why the neighbors respected Ed and asked for his help at times. Ed was always willing to help them, whether it be a small loan or cutting some firewood for them, he never seemed to turn anyone down. This made Charlie proud and respectful towards his new dad. And it also offset the hurt feelings he felt when kids said something about his mother had worked in a bar and he didn't have a real father. Well now his mother didn't have to work long hard hours in a restaurant or a bar, and he secretly hoped she would never have to again. And if they didn't believe his real father had died, well they didn't have to. Not everything on the farm was a bed of roses though. Some of Charlie's young calves became sick and went into convulsions. Papa Locker, the local veterinarian was called out, but couldn't determine what the cause was until him and Charlie saw one of the other calves eating fallen Almond blossoms from one of the Almond trees. He lost three calves from this, so Ed helped him put wire fences around the five Almond trees in the pasture.

The night they were going to tell Ed about the baby coming, he came home from the milk route late. They had two trucks now and one of them had broken down, and Ed had to repair it along the road. He was tired, dirty and hungry. He washed his face and hands and sit down to a warmed over dinner, Naomer and Charlie sat down at the table with him. Naomer touched his arm.

"Ed, I have some good news to tell ya." Naomer hesitated awhile. "We're going ta have a baby."

"A real baby," Charlie added with excitement.

Ed smiled quietly and continued eating. "When's it coming?" he asked, and took another mouth full of food.

"The end of August probably," answered Naomer. "I recon we better start getting prepared for the little one."

"Yeah, you better go buy it a crib and buggy," Ed added.

"I can make most of the baby clothes and diapers and blankets for it, but first I need to borrow a sewing machine."

"What can I do for it?" Charlie asked.

"You can help me make it a high chair as soon as I have time to start on it," Ed told him.

Charlie beamed. He would be proud to help Ed make a highchair for the new baby. He and his mother actually had a family.

"Come on Venture. Let's go to bed, girl. Have to get up early to get the chores done before school. Night Mom and Dad," he said as he headed towards the bedroom with Venture following close behind. Venture was part of their family too, he thought, as he hugged her close.

That summer of 1943 was an exciting one for Charlie. Most of his time was spent at the river when he wasn't taking care of his animals or working the late afternoons at the feed store. He and Venture would walk half a mile to the river where some of his boy friends were always there swimming. He loved the warm sandy beaches and the cold water on a hot summer day. Venture would swim out half way across the river before she would turn around and swim back. Then she would shake vigorously and roll over and over in the sand. The boys were always hollering for her to get away and stop shaking water and sand all over them.

Charlie and his friends didn't worry too much about the war that was still going on, but they did discuss things they heard their parents say about it. Some of the boys said their parents wish the war would end and some parents thought the United States should take more responsibility in the war, more aggression to bring it to an end.

"I wish I was old enough to go fight in the war," one of his friends said.

"Me too," several of the other boys agreed.

Charlie just wanted to enjoy his new family before he grew up, and continue raising the animals on the farm he had longed for so long.

Summer finally came to an end. The boys were getting bored of hanging out at the river after three months. Shopping for new school clothes and getting ready for football practice became the main topics of their conversation. Charlie had to stay home more now and help his mother around the house because it was getting close for the arrival of the baby. Naomer had all the baby clothes and diapers made. She didn't have to buy a sewing machine because an older neighbor, Grandma Duvas, who had become very special to the family, loaned Naomer her machine as she didn't use it very much anymore. They had bought a new crib and buggy, and Ed with Charlie's help was making the high chair in the evenings when they had time.

Here in California most of the women now went to the hospital for their babies to be born. All arrangements were made at a hospital in Lodi, all that was left was for the baby to make it's appearance.

When her labor pains started at three o'clock in the morning. Ed woke Charlie and they all traveled to the hospital on the east side of town. Unfortunately, Naomer's regular doctor was out of town and his young assistant had to see her.

"I believe you're just having some false labor pains, Naomer," he told her. It doesn't look like that baby is ready to come yet. Maybe he's waiting for Dr. Lance to get back," he joked. "I think you could just go back home and try to get some sleep. Might not get much sleep after the little fella gets here."

"These pains are pretty bad, but if ya don't think I'm ready, guess I'll go home. Sure would like ta get it over with though," Naomer told him."

"Dr. Lance will be back late this afternoon. I don't think the baby will come before than," the young doctor said, while he cleaned his glasses on the end of his medical jacket.

The pains went away for awhile, but started again in the late morning. Naomer tried to ignore them, but they finally got so severe about one o'clock she told Ed he better take her back to the hospital.

Ed had already run his morning milk route and Charlie had stayed at home with Naomer that morning. They headed back to the hospital hoping this time the baby would be born. The young doctor examined Naomer again, puzzled about the pains, because it seemed the baby still wasn't coming. By the time Dr. Lance arrived at the hospital Naomer was having severe pains and cramps. He took one look at her and hollered to the nurses to take her to delivery.

"The cords around the baby's neck," Naomer heard him say, just as she drifted off from the mask the nurse had quickly placed over her face. Ed and Charlie had been ushered out to the waiting room when Naomer had been taken into the delivery room.

"Will Momma be alright?" Charlie asked Ed.

"Sure, your momma will be okay," Ed assured him.

"And the baby?" asked Charlie.

"Don't know, Charlie. I sure hope it's alright," answered Ed.

Charlie took Ed's hand and together they waited for what seemed like an eternity, but was only thirty seven minutes before the nurse came out and said they had a fine baby boy and Naomer was resting just fine.

"You'll be able to see the baby through the nursery window in a while," the nurse said, as she motioned her hand towards the hallway to the left. "Just follow the hall on down."

Charlie and Ed looked in the nursery window. There were three babies in small cribs inside. Two girls in pink and a boy in blue. They read the name tag on the boy, but it was not theirs. A few minutes later a nurse brought a baby into the nursery and held it up for them to see. A lot of dark hair covered it's little head, while dark eyes seem to look at them through the window.

"Are we still going to call him Carl after Grandpa in Alabama?" asked Charlie, as he looked at the glow on Ed's face.

"Think so," answered Ed, "Edward Carl ."

Time passed quickly with a new baby in the house and all the animals to take care of. Charlie stopped going to the river as it had began to get boring by the end of summer. He was glad that school was starting and fall was coming. He would be in the sixth grade and was allowed to play football and baseball with the older boys now.

He hurried through the front door after school on a late October day with a puppy following close behind. "Momma, this pup followed me home. I don't think he belongs to anyone. Can I keep him?" Charlie pleaded while he opened the refrigerator and got a piece of baloney from a wrapper, giving the puppy bites of it until it was all gone.

Naomer looked up from her ironing, eyeing the pup while it begged for more baloney. "Well, my heavens, Charlie, ya got so many animals now, ya don't really need another one."

"But Venture is getting old and she don't like to play much anymore," he offered.

"Well, she'll be jealous of that pup, won't ya Venture," she asked, as Venture walked up to the pup smelling him.

"Aw promise I won't neglect Venture, Momma. She can play with him too."

"You better find out first if he belongs to anyone," Naomer told him. "He looks like he's got wolf in him. What if he kills your chickens and ducks?"

"Aw'll train him not too," was Charlie's reply while he led the pup to a corner in the kitchen where Venture's water was kept. I'll take him back to where he started following me and see if he belongs to anyone there."

An old man, who Charlie stopped and talked to quite often, told him that the pup had been hanging around there for several days. "Someone probably dropped him off here. Take him on home, son, he's yours. Nobody around here wants him."

So Charlie kept the pup, calling him just 'Wolf'. Wolf glowed in the attention Charlie gave him, while Venture wasn't too sure whether she liked sharing Charlie with another dog. But than Wolf was fun to play with outside when Charlie was gone and she felt like playing. They chased each other, and played keep-a-way with a short rope or stick, whatever they could find. Venture would sometimes creep slowly toward Wolf while he tucked his tail at first, cowarding, not knowing if Venture was playing or going to attack him. But he soon learned it was only play and would creep towards her until they met, than off they would go on a chase of each other around the yard. Venture was amazed at Wolf's long tail, as her's was docked at birth. She would grab his tail and he would spin around to get away.

Charlie went with Ed one early Saturday morning on the milk route. A farmer on the route told them he had lost a mare with milk fever and she had a foal he was trying to raise on the bottle. He said he would like to sell the colt because he didn't have time to feed him.

"What do ya want for that foal, mister?" asked Charlie when he heard this.

"Well, aw don't rightly know. He's a fine colt. Comes from some good bloodlines," the man told him, and spit his tobacco into the soft dirt.

"Well, aw got a new litter of pigs. Whould you trade him for two pigs," ask Charlie.

"Tell ya what, son, you can have him for four pigs and take him home right now," the farmer said.

"Well, I'll trade you three pigs and take him home right now," Charlie bargained.

The man studied the ground for awhile, "Okay, three pigs. We got a deal. I'll even give ya the bottle I made for him. It's only a soda pop bottle with a rubber glove finger, but he nurses it pretty darn good."

So Charlie led the three week old colt the three miles to home, while Ed continued on his route. At times the colt balked, but Charlie held the bottle up full of milk and he continued to follow. By the time they reached home, they were both pretty wore out, but the colt had started bonding with Charlie and from than on considered Charlie his 'new momma'.

Ed helped him build a stall for the colt in the old barn so he would have shelter for the coming winter. They named him Tony and started him on some grain, but continued bottle feeding him with milk from a nanny goat which Charlie had also acquired from someone wanting to get rid of the goat.

Charlie rigged a halter up for Tony with some old ropes and taught him to lead without the bottle. He filled out nicely through the winter after Charlie wormed him and brushed him almost everyday.

Winter passed and spring arrived suddenly with green grass in the pastures, wild flowers and new life sprouting up all over Charlie's farm. New chicks and ducks were running around the hugh fenced in area.

Baby Ed was crawling, trying to get into everything. Naomer was pregnant again, with a due date the end of November. Charlie helped with little Ed as much as he could. But with all his animals to feed in the morning and still working at the feed store the two hours after school, then feeding everything again in the evening, he really did keep busy.

Naomer still did ironing for people and helped Charlie butcher the rabbits when he had customers for them. She had a lot of nice neighbor ladies around town that she visited with. They helped each other wall paper and paint their homes and baby sit for each other's children.

People were still having a hard time making a living after the depression. And so many of the young husbands were away at war. Most people just had enough to survive on, but for Ed and Naomer the milk route did very well, and they had a much better living than most folks. Ed added on a bathroom to their home to replace the old one outside. They were able to buy a new refrigerator and do away with the old ice box. Charlie missed the ice man coming in the summertime, because he always gave Charlie a big chunk of ice if he was home. Charlie broke it up with an ice pick and shared it with Venture and Wolf on the lawn.

The war continued and D Day took place on June 6, 1944. Normandy was invaded according to the radio announcer and America and her allies joined forces in the greatest military strength ever assembled. The war was always the formost thing on all grownup American minds. The radio played a big part in the American life----bringing news of the war everyday. Once in awhile when Charlie was able to go to a movie in Lodi where he saw the newsreels about the war on the huge screen. It was exciting he felt, but yet scary. So many service men were getting killed, even a few Charlie had known from his small town of Lockeford.

That summer he hung out with his boyfriends again at the river on hot afternoons. Venture and Wolf always followed along with him and found a shade tree to lie under after a swim in the cool water. When the boys got hungry the ate the peaches and nectarines in the near by orchards. The farmers didn't care that the boys ate the fruit if they didn't break any branches or leave litter on the ground.

The boys always waited awhile to swim after they ate, except for Ronnie who didn't believe you couldn't swim right after you eat. One particular day after they all ate peaches he took off swimming across the river.

"I got cramps, help," he hollered, when he was about halfway across the river.

The boys watched him, thinking he was just kidding them. But then he went under the water and came up floundering.

"I think he really is in trouble," one of the boys said.

All four boys took off to save Ronnie. The boys swan out, but the river was so swift at that center point, that they couldn't swim fast enough to reach him as the current carried him down stream. Charlie called Venture and Wolf. The dogs ran to the edge of the water waiting for a command.

"Fetch, fetch," Charlie hollered and pointed to the struggling swimmer.

The dogs ran on down the beach getting ahead of Ronnie who was still hollering for help, but starting to fight less and loosing consciousness. The dogs swam out, Venture getting to the victim first, grabbing hold of his arm and turning back toward the beach while Wolf grabbed hold of his other arm, they swiftly pulled him onto the beach. The boys swam back to the beach and quickly ran to Ronnie turning him on his stomache giving him artificial respiration. He came to coughing and chocking, but seemed to be alright in a short while.

"Guess I won't get in that cold water just after I eat again," he said "thanks for saving my life."

"Well, it was Venture and Wolf that really saved you," one of the boys said.

"Thanks dogs," he said and patted them while they licked his arm, like they understood what he had said.

The whole town heard about the dogs saving Ronnie from drowning and were hero's for awhile until the episode was forgotten.

Wolf did have one bad habit. He liked to follow Naomer's car when she went somewhere. Perhaps because the 1942 Plymonth had a smitty for the muffler and made a loud noice. He would follow her to the grocery store, except instead of running after the car he would run along the river bottom land and circle around to the store to meet her there. Then while she went into the store to do her shopping he thought he should protect her by sitting at the front door and not letting anyone enter. Looking very much like a wolf people were naturally afraid of him, especially when he showed his teeth and growled low at them. Naomer would have to quit her shopping and go scold Wolf and send him home. The town constable tried to make Wolf leave the front of he store once and almost got bit, so Naomer tried to remember to always tie Wolf up when she had to go somewhere after that.

One day though Wolf got untied. This time he took Highway 88 which ran right through the middle of Lockeford a half mile to the grocery store. Naomer had just paid for her sack of groceries when a lady friend rushed into the store.

"Naomer, your wolf dog was just hit by a lumber truck. Here, I'll take the baby and the groceries to your car and you go see about him." Her friend said.

Naomer hurried the half block to Wolf laying on the left side of the road. She was getting big with her second child due in only two months. The truck that hit him had not stopped, but several town people were standing near by and a shop owner that Naomer knew came out when he saw her run up to the dog.

"Naomer, wait let me hep you," the man said, as he hurried over to her.

"Oh he's not moving. Am afraid he's dead," she exclaimed, as they rolled Wolf gently over on his side. They both kneeled down closer to feel for a heart beat.

"There's no life," the man said, as he moved his hand over Wolf's chest.

"Oh, whatever will aw tell Charlie. He loved that dog so much," she said with tears in her eyes.

"Well, I'm sure he'll understand," the man answered. "If you drive your car over here, I'll get some newspapers in my shop and put in your car trunk to lay the dog on," he said as he moved the dog farther off the roadside.

"Thank you so much for helping," Naomer said.

Charlie took this bad. He didn't blame anyone. It was just Wolf. He always liked to rome if the family was gone, he would jump over the fence. Charlie was glad that Venture liked to stay home in her yard, and didn't follow Wolf when he would leave. Charlie dug a big hole in the back yard to bury Wolf, with Venture by his side watching every move. He patted Wolf, "Goodbye old friend." Venture whined as though she knew Wolf wouldn't be with them anymore. No more romps in the yard with Wolf or chasing rabbits in the bottom land, or laying on the sandy beach after a cool swim in the river.

"We love you Wolf, you had such a short life, only over a year," Charlie said, with tears streaming down his face. Charlie shoveled dirt into the hole and put the cross on top that he had made with two pieces of wood, and added some artificial flowers to it that his mother had given him. He said a short prayer ending with "Please take care of Wolf, Jesus."

1944

A baby girl, Carlene Rose, was born to Naomer that November. Charlie and Ed were thrilled. Their family was certainly growing, and Christmas that year was the best he could ever remember. They drove up into the mountains to Murphys and cut a six foot spruce tree to decorate. A light snow covered the landscape, making it glisten as the bright sun reflected over it.

They stopped for a few moments at the Tone Ranch to wish everyone there a Merry Christmas and to show the babies off. The Tones were all very happy to see Charlie and to know his wish for a family had finally come true.

Charlie was up early Christmas morning. He looked out the window to see if it had snowed. He was hoping it would for Christmas, but they hardly ever got any snow in the San Joaquin Valley. It was cold though and frost was on the windows. Charley put more wood into the stove and made enough noise that he hoped would wake up the rest of the family so they could open the gifts.

Little Edward woke up and standing in his crib hollered, "up Charlie, up Charlie." Charlie finally went to get him after several calls and let him run around in his pajamas and his squeaky mouse house shoes, while trying to keep him out of the presents. Baby Rose started crying and Naomer got up to fix her a bottle. This woke Ed who knew the family would be waiting to open all the presents under the tree. He had already went out on his route earlier that morning and returned back home, filling the stove with wood before he crawled back into bed. He knew the family would be up early to celebrate Christmas.

"Charlie, you hand the gifts out," Ed said, as he sat down holding Edward on his lap and Naomer held Rose while she had her bottle. After he gave Carl a gift to open, Charlie handed one to his mother that was a pretty store wrapped gift from woolworths where he had done all his shopping. "Momma, open this one," he said. "Here Dad, is your gift from me.

"Oh, Charlie, just what I needed, a bottle of Blue Waltz Cologne," Naomer said as she sprayed a little on her, being careful to spray away from the baby. "What did you get, Ed?" she asked, as he held up a small pocket knife.

"Thanks, Charlie, I need a new knife."

After the gifts were all opened there was stuffed animals, toys and wrapping paper everywhere. Even Venture got a sack full of toys and dog biscuits. Charlie's favorite gift was a new Red Ryder BB Gun.

"Well now, I'll just fix us a special Christmas breakfast," Naomer told the family and got up to put the sleeping baby in her crib.

Edward played with his new toys while Charlie and Ed picked up all the Christmas paper and bows scattered all over the living room. They sat down to thick waffles with homemade strawberry jam, scrambled eggs and crisp bacon, while Christmas carols played on the radio.

Throughout the day family and neighbors dropped by to bring presents or just to wish them a Merry Christmas. Naomer thought a lot about her family in Alabama, especially at the holidays. She slipped away to the bedroom while Ed and Charlie was listening to a program on the radio and the babies were sleeping. Tears were in her eyes as she thought of her mother dying so young. She missed her so much and knew her sisters must miss her terribly too. Willer Mae was twenty now and had married several years ago to an older man. Maggie had four children now, but Francis had not been able to have children. Naomer's father, Carl, had married a women with two daughters. R.T., who was divorced from his first wife, had married the oldest daughter. A cute slender girl with light brown hair according to the photos and letters they had sent Naomer.

Charlie's family listened to the news on the war everyday, as did most other American families that had a radio. The United States Marines landed on Iwo Jima in February of 1945. It was a bloody battle there and lives were lost everyday. The eight square miles of Iwa Jima, which consisted mostly of volcanic rock and ash was defended by the Japanese. The United State troops had no cover while the Japanese watched their every move from any point of the island. Also that February, President Franklin D. Roosevelt, British Prime Minister, Winston S. Churchill, and Soviet Premier Josef Stalin, met at a conference to plan the United Nations. Fifty one countries were invited to the meeting to make the final plans. A Charter would be signed to keep world peace and develop friendly relations among the nations to solve problems.

Charlie and his friends played war games a lot. With all the grownups talking about the war constantly, it only seemed natural that they would pretend to play war. If five or six joined into play they divided up into countries. One group was always the Americans and the other would be Germany, Japan or some foreign country.

One particular time Charlie found a German flag in his parent's closet that belonged to Ed's family. "Look what I found," he told the boys as he unfolded the flag on the lawn in his front yard.

"Wow! A real German flag!" his friend Ronnie exclaimed. "Let's put it on a pole."

"Where's the American flag?" one of the boys ask.

"Right here," answered Charlie. "Let's put the German flag on that tall pole where everyone can see it," refering to an electrical pole in the front yard close to the road.

"Yeah, and the American flag on that tall tree," another boy said, pointing to a tall Oak Tree.

After the war games were over the boys were tired and ready to go home. The decided to leave the flags up so they could play again tomorrow.

That evening a deputy from the County Sheriff's Office knocked on Charlie's front door.

"Evening Mame," the deputy said to Naomer when she opened the door.

"Good Evening, Sir."

"Mame, do you know you have a German flag flying from that pole in your yard?" he asked, as he pointed to the pole.

"No officer, I sure didn't?" Naomer looked up at the flag flapping in the gentle breeze.

"Well Mame, did you know it's against the law to fly a German flag? Now who do you suppose put it up here?" he asked.

"Well probably my son. He and his friends play war a lot."

"Can I talk to him, Mame?"

"Yes sir. Charlie come here," she called to him. "Charlie did you and the boys put that German flag on the pole in the front."

"Yes, so's we could play war."

"Well son, it's against the law to fly a German flag in the United States," the law officer told him. "Now can you take it down immediately before we have any more complaints and before the military officers decide to come out here," he laugh in a friendly way. "That can cause a lot of trouble for your family if the wrong people see it," the officer continued.

Charlie's friends couldn't believe that a Deputy Sheriff came out because of them flying the German flag, when he told them at school the next day. The rumor was all over town. Some people thought it to be funny while others frowned on it. Ed's family was very upset over it. But it was soon forgotten.

Tony was almost full grown by now and would soon be a two year old colt, ready to break and train. Ed had talked about having his friend to train him, but Charlie was anxious to start breaking the colt himself. Charlie had never broke a horse before, but watched "ole Smoky" at the movies and other westerns that showed how the cowboys did it and figured he could do the same with Tony. So one day when his folks had gone to town shopping for the day, he took Tony down to the soft dirt at the river bottom. He had already been putting a saddle on him, so Tony was pretty use to the saddle by now. Charlie climbed aboard the fifteen hands high horse. Tony liked Charlie, still linking him to the only mother he remembered. After all, Charlie had bottle fed him and nurtured him since he was just a few weeks old, but to have a weight on his back was another story with the colt.

From a distance Charlie noticed one of the neighbors watching him. He hoped he wouldn't tell his folks. D.S. was a good natured intelligent man that Charlie had become close too. He was probably just watching him in case he got hurt, Charlie thought, but he still wished he would go back into his house. In case he fell off, Charlie didn't particularly want someone to see him in that embarrassing moment.

D.S. was half Indian. He had been raised on a reservation and had a lot of interesting stories to tell about those days and the beliefs of the Indians. In his sixties now, he walked with a limp because his horse had tripped in a Prairie Dog hole, falling and throwing D.S. off causing his hip to break as a teenager.

The colt bucked several short hard bucks, but Charlie held on to the saddle horn with one hand and the reins with the other. The colt stopped suddenly and just stood there not knowing what to do. Charlie kicked him gently with his legs and he crow hopped several feet and stood there again not knowing what Charlie wanted.

D.S. walked across the two acres of land. "Let me help you, son," he told Charlie, "I've broke a lot of young foals in my lifetime. This colt likes you because you're the only friend he's ever had, but he's a little spoiled. You need to ground break him first. Get off and I'll show you how," the dark complexioned man told Charlie.

He took the reins and tied a light rope he had brought with him to each end of the reins to make them longer. Getting behind the horse with a long rein on each side he could control which way he wanted the horse to go.

"See son, it's easier to control him from behind and the horse has less tension without a rider on his back yet, and can give more thought to going right or left. Git up, Tony," D.S. said as he gently snapped the reins. The colt went forward about twenty feet until D.S. pulled the reins back and hollered "Whoa, Whoa, boy." The colt stopped. D.S. showed Charlie how to turn him right and left.

"Now just practice this for about a week. Then get on him, and I don't think you'll have any problem. Won't be long and you'll be running these fields on him."

"Thank you, D.S., aw sure appreciate this," Charlie told him, taking hold of the reins.

For a week Charlie practiced reining Tony forward, back, right and left. When he did get on his back the colt knew what he wanted and seemed to pick it up without any trouble. About three weeks after Charlie's first attempt at riding Tony the friend of Ed's came over to break him. Now Charlie hadn't told his folks yet that he had been riding him down in the bottom land for fear they would be mad because they were afraid he would get hurt. The cowboy called Slim, gently put the saddle on Tony and softly put his left foot in the stirrup swinging ever so lightly up in the saddle. The horse started bucking hard, wanting nothing to do with this tall stranger on his back. He bucked until the cowboy fell off. Charlie was watching all of this, not knowing if he should tell his folks who were also standing by watching, that he had already started riding the colt with D.S.'s help. Slim dusted himself off and climbed on the horse again, only to get bucked off again. Just as Charlie started to tell his folks, D.S. walked into the pasture.

You're a ruining that horse by fighting him," D.S. said, "This young'n here's been riding that colt for two weeks now. Get on him son, and show em," he told Charlie.

Slim, Ed and Naomer watched with their mouths open while Charlie got on Tony and rode him around in the pasture. Charlie felt big because he had broke his own colt, of course with the help of D.S. However, he did get grounded for a week from riding the horse and from playing with his friends because of disobeying.

Charlie rode Tony everywhere. They were best of friends, and Venture learned that Tony wouldn't hurt Charlie when he rode him and she followed along with them. Tony even followed Charlie out on the sloping Oak tree trunk and on to the diving board that the boys had put up at the river.

All that summer Tony noticed the beautiful mares grazing in a field near the river. They belonged to the race horse ranch there. Tony held his head high to get their scent and curled his upper lip while Charlie and the boys laugh at him. Several times Charlie had to go get Tony when they were at the river because he would venture over to the fence by the mares, The mares always came running to him and would whinny inviting him to join them. Charlie would get there just before Tony had a chance to jump the fence, and would than tie him to a tree branch close to the river. One time Tony broke the diving board when he was following Charlie out to dive and all the boys were mad at Charlie for this. He had to buy another diving board and had a time keeping Tony off of it.

Charlie and the colt were both as wild as the wind when they rode, jumping fences and shrubs, and more than once Charlie ended up with broken bones. In late summer the manager of the race horse ranch came by Charlie's small farm to talk to him. The ranch raised some of the fastest race horses on the west coast. He found Charlie out back doing his chores and waved to him. Charlie walked toward him.

"Hello, son. You got a mighty nice little farm here," he told him. Bet it keeps you busy."

"Yeah, it does," he answered, eyeing the man curiously. He knew who he was, but wondered what he was doing here. The man took his baseball cap off and stroked his graying hair.

Son, I was wondering if you'd be interested in selling that colt of yours?" he asked.

"Aw don't think so sir. Me and him's pretty close," answered Charlie, wondering why this man would be interested in Tony. He didn't have racing bloodlines.

"Aw don't think he's got any racing blood in him, sir," Charlie said, wiping his sweaty forehead with his shirt.

"Well, I'd give you a good price for him, son. How would two hundred dollars be?"

"That would be pretty good, Mr. Lewis, but I rightly don't want to sale him."

"You know, son, your horse is lonesome. You've had to come and get him a number of times when he almost jumped the fences to get over to the mares.

Now we can't have him jumping over the fences and getting in with those ten thousand dollar mares," Mr. Lewis said. He than continued with some anger in his voice, "You either geld him or sell him to me. Tell you what, you talk it over with your dad and let me know in a few days."

That night at the supper table Charlie told his folks about the visit of the race horse ranch manager.

"My goodness, that's a lot of money for that horse. Maybe you should consider it, son. I'm afraid you're gonna get hurt real bad on him someday. You've already broke your arm twice on him," Naomer went on.

"Do you know what they'll do to that horse? They don't want him. They'll take him out back and shoot him and send him to the glue factory. They don't want him breeding those mares," Ed said.

"Oh is that what it is?" ask Naomer, as she put a spoonful of mashed potatoes into the baby's mouth.

"Why of course," Ed went on, "You don't think they want some two bit horse for a racing ranch?"

"He's not a two bit horse," Charlie broke in. He's a good horse, and he's my friend and they can't have him."

"Well, I know you didn't want to geld him, Charlie, but I suppose you better now. And try to break him from jumping those fences," Ed added, and dipped his bread in the last bit of gravy on his plate.

Old Doc Locker came out and gelded Tony before Mr. Lewis came by a week later. He was glad to hear the colt was gelded and was also happy that Charlie was going to try to break him from jumping fences.

Tony started feeling better, but still had the mares on his mind. It was Saturday and Charlie was going to try to break him from jumping fences. Ed had mentioned several times that someone should pepper him with some rock salt when Tony reared up on the fences. This should break him of that, Ed had said.

So when Tony started running around close to the fences like he was anticipating jumping over, Charlie fired a shot at him from behind a tree where he was hiding with the 12 gauge shot gun. Tony screamed and took off in a gallope towards the barn. Charlie not thinking anymore about it went on about his work and play. That evening when he fed Tony he checked him underneath and noticed he was very very swollen. Charlie told Ed what he had done and Ed checked the colt and called the veterinarian.

Ole Doc Locker was pretty mad at Charlie when he found out he had peppered the colt with rock salt underneath where his surgery had been. Ed explained to Charlie he had been to close to the colt when he fired at him.

"You needed to fire farther away, then it would of just scared him," Ed told him.

Charlie couldn't ride Tony for about three weeks, but it did seem like he was a better horse now since the gelding and the rock salt and he didn't try to jump the fences ever again.

The two were inseparable. Charlie rode Tony all over Lockeford and out in the country. He even rode him to school and put him in a stall in the old barn, where the children left their horses while they attended classes.

One Saturday morning Charlie was riding him close to the railroad tracks when a train came through. Charlie thought it might be fun to try to out run it. He kicked Tony in the sides and hollered "git up, boy," slapping the reins from side to side. The train, with about ten cars and a caboose was going fast, and Charlie and Tony were getting further behind. All of a sudden the train began to slow and finally came to a stop. Charlie rode on up to the caboose to see what was happening.

"Son, are you trying to stop the train? Is something wrong?" the engineer asked.

"Oh no, sir, aw was just trying to race you," answered Charlie.

The engineer looked very angry. "Well don't you know that's dangerous trying to race a train? I ought'a come down there and spank your behind. Don't you ever race a train again."

Charlie went home. He had not met to cause any harm, he only wanted to see if Tony could outrun the train.

D.S. had a son a few years older than Charlie. They got along good most of the time, but Derald had loaned Charlie his sling shot and he had lost it. Derald being older, liked to tease Charlie, especially when some of the older boys were around.

Charlie, if you don't find my sling shot I'm gonna burn your ducks alive," Derald warned him.

"You wouldn't dare," Charlie hollered back at him, and turned walking back towards his house to listen to one of his favorite radio programs while his family was away for the afternoon.

A half hour later Charlie heard Derald calling him. "Hey Charlie, watch your ducks."

Charlie scrambled to the door and saw Derald in his back pasture pouring something over one of his ducks as it waddled by the edge of the pond. He hurried out across the back yard to the pasture as Derald lit a match to a piece of paper and threw it on the duck. The duck took off flying but was soon engulfed with flames and plopped back to the ground. Derald took off for home. His folks were also gone that day and he knew Charlie couldn't tell on him. Charlie picked the dead duck up and threw it in the burning barrel where he finished burning it so that it wouldn't smell, all the while thinking of a way to get even with Derald.

A few days later he slipped over to Derald's house about the time he knew they were sitting down to supper. He pulled two hot peppers from the garden out of his pocket and coaxed Derald's goat up to the back screen door with them. He gently opened the door still coaxing the goat to go inside. Then he stuffed the hot peppers in the goat's mouth and pushed him towards the kitchen. Charlie slipped back out the door and hid behind an old abandoned stove in the yard.

Quite soon he heard the family scream and someone holler, "The goats went mad. He's foaming at the mouth."

Charlie could hear the goat running into things and a loud crash, while the family scrambled around trying to get the goat out of the house. He thought this was a good time to disappear before anyone saw him.

The early teen years always causes mischievous behavior in boys, and Charlie was sure no exception. One of Naomer's friends called her saying she saw Charlie and a friend sitting up town on the sidewalk in Lockeford and they were sick. Naomer left the babies with a neighbor and hurried down town to see what was wrong. She found them in the ally vomiting and moaning.

"Charlie, what in the world's wrong with you?" she asked, noticing they reeked of wine. "Have you boys been drinking wine?"

"Yeah, Donald stoled it from his dad's wine cellar," Charlie answered. "Mom, I'm sorry. Just take us home please," he begged.

Naomer got the boys into her car and dropped Donald off at his home before taking Charlie home and getting him in the shower and than to bed. He was grounded for several weeks and vowed to never have another drink of wine.

The war still continued. Every night the family sat around the radio listening to the news of the war. On August 6, 1945 the radio blared out that the United States had dropped an Atomic Bomb on Hiroshima, Japan at quarter past eight Japan time. Harry S. Truman was President, and the ending war was the upper most thing on everyone's mind. Than on October 24, 1945. Enough countries had signed the agreement called the 'Charter'. To form the United Nations, which would help to keep world peace and solve problems among nations.

Another baby boy, James Godfried, was born to Naomer the following January. Charlie secretly hoped this would be the last one. Three was more than he bargained for, but he loved each one and was devoted to helping take care of them.

That spring Charlie had to start driving one of the milk trucks with a temporary driving permit. Ed's driver that had been on the truck, came down with a chronic illness and had to quite working. Not another driver could be found, as the war had made such a shortage of men at home. Most men and women were working in the factories, and the service men had not all come home yet, even though the war had ended. So Charlie was issued a special driving work licenses by the Department of Motor Vehicles.

He had cut down on raising rabbits, and had sold the rest of his calves and pigs last fall. The farm work was less, but he had to get up around four in the morning to go on the milk route. He had to be on the route seven days a week morning and evening. After the morning route was finished, he came home to eat breakfast and get ready to go to school, which started at nine o'clock.

Naomer wanted Ed to sell the milk trucks and route and take a regular eight hour a day job. Seven days a week was taking its toll on Ed, and now Charlie at fourteen was trying to keep up with him. They had made good money over the last few years and was able to save some, and Naomer thought they should quit working so hard. She was also begging Ed for them all to take a trip back to Alabama to see her family. It had been almost nine years since she had left Alabama and last seen her family there, and she was very homesick. Charlie too was anxious to see his grandpa and aunts and uncle.

In early fall after the milk route and trucks were sold, Ed bought a brand new 1946 Chevrolet, and they headed to Alabama in it. D.S. and Derald would take care of Venture, Tony and the other animals for the three weeks that they would be gone. Charlie would miss the first weeks of school, but everyone said the education of the trip would more than compensate for lost school time.

The trip took four long driving days. Ed and Naomer took turns driving and sleeping, and they all entertained the children. The children were good, and the humming motor of the new Chevy lulled them to sleep more than they normally would have slept at home. They had books and games to play with and Charlie taught the Three and two year old how to count the cars and the horses and cows in the pastures along the way. They did stop late at night at a motel and had baths, and a hot supper at a near by restaurant.

On the road early the next morning they had fruit for breakfast brought from home and usually baloney and cheese sandwiches made along the way for dinner.

Naomer's whole family had moved to the Birmingham area several years before in search of better paying jobs. Her father, Carl, had obtained a job as a steel worker with Virginia Bridge. When they crossed the Alabama border they stopped at a filling station for gas and Naomer called her family from a pay phone to tell them where they were at and when they would arrive.

"Oh Daddy, it's so good to hear ya voice this close. We'll be there in a couple hours."

"Well Honey, a'm a gonna call in sick today so's aw can be here when ya'll arrive," he told her. "Do ya have the directions to the house. It's in kind of a run down part of town, but that's about all we could afford when we came here."

"We'll find it, Daddy," Naomer assured him.

When they arrived, Safronie, Naomer's new step mother, had a noon meal on the table. After everyone was introduced and a lot of hugs went around, they all sat down and Carl gave the thanks for their safe trip and the delicious looking home cooked food of potatoe salad, poke salad greens and fried pork chops, followed by sweet potatoe pie. It was appreciated after restaurant and cold food all week.

"Ya'll's babies are so sweet," Safronie said to Naomer, "Aw sure bet they keep ya busy."

"Oh they sure do," laugh Naomer, looking at her three and two year olds who had dark brown hair and dark eyes, and the baby who had blond hair and blue eyes.

Safronie had borrowed a high chair and little Edward sat in that, while Ed held Rose and fed her, and Naomer held the nine month old, feeding him some sweet potatoe pie along with his jar of baby food.

Naomer's new step sister, Alice, asked if she could hold the baby after he ate so that Naomer could finish her dinner. Naomer eyed Alice couriously. She was a tiny little thing. She thought Carl had told her that

Alice was only nine when he and Safronie got married, so that would make her about thirteen, Naomer surmised. She had light brown hair and was very petite, taking after her mother. And of course, Naomer heard the other daughter, Gladyes, that was R.T's. wife now, was also tiny and petite.

"Well, Charlie, we all heard so much about ya when ya were a little tyke from your grandpa and Willer Mae," Safronie said, "Aw didn't expect ya to be so grown up."

"Na, aw sure didn't either. But he's still got that there red curly hair and freckles," Carl smiled, and put his arm around Charlie's shoulders.

In the early evening after the babies had their naps, Charlie and his family drove out to the farm where Francis and her husband, Roy, lived and where they share cropped. Naomer and Francis held each other and cried until little Rose started crying from all the commotion. Naomer swooped her up.

"This is your Auntie Francis. Can ya give her kisses?"

Rose clung to Naomer, eyeing Aunt Francis very couriously.

"Roy and aw want kids so bad, but aw just don't seem to git pregnant," Francis pitifully told Naomer. "Here ya'll are blessed with three beautiful babies and Charlie too," she went on.

"Well, I don't plan to have any more," Naomer announced. "And you all will have some one of these days." Look how long it took me to have the last three. Why Charlie thought he was never gonna get a brother or sister.

Francis hugged Charlie, "Oh my little Charles Thomas. Aw can't believe you're almost all grown up now."

Roy took Ed and Charlie fishing the next day while Naomer and Francis stayed home with the babies and did a lot of reminiscing.

"Aw miss Momma so much," Naomer said.

"me too," answered Francis.

"It just ain't the same without her. Was it really her heart, Francis? I didn't even know she had heart trouble.

"It was her heart alright. But aw really believe Momma didn't know she had heart trouble till just a few weeks before she died. Pa just got ta where he drank an awful lot, and him and Momma would get in some terrible fights. Aw think she was under a lot of stress. Well, ya don't need to be a hearing all this stuff, sis. Aw don't want ta talk anymore about it."

Naomer wiped her eyes, "I should of never went to California. Daddy would always listen to me when I told him to leave Mamma alone. I should of stayed here and protected her. He hadn't drink much for along time before I left though and I thought he had quite, Well I never should have left her. She didn't want me too."

"Now don't go a blaming yourself, sis. It was just met for Momma to go. It was her time and you couldn't of stopped it. The good Lord knows," Francis said.

"Does Daddy still drink?" Naomer asked.

"Not as much. Safronie is good for him. And am sure he blames hisself a lot for Momma's death, but won't admit it to anyone."

That evening Carl, Safronie and Alice joined the family while Roy and some friends played Ho Down music on their front porch. Roy was a fine fiddler and had even played at the Grand Ole Opery. Several neighbors dropped over with guitars, fiddles and banjos , and everyone sit outside playing and singing till late in the night.

Charlie had never done anything like this before, and thought it was great. He had never had the time to take lessons with an instrument, but thought he just might do that when he got back home. There were several cute neighbor girls there also and they glanced at Charlie from time to time.

Naomer smiled at Ed who was talking quietly with her dad and several men while they listened to the music. She was afraid he wouldn't fit in with the men here as his ways were so different, but he really seemed to be enjoying himself and relaxing for the first time in months.

The next day they followed Francis and Roy in their car over to Willer Mae's house which was deep in the woods. Willer Mae had married a man about ten years older than her. Everyone called him "Nin," They didn't have any children either and this brought them together a lot with Francis and Roy.

Willer Mae was so happy to see her big sister, Naomer, and she hugged Charlie until he thought she was never going to release him. Willer Mae still seemed the same as when she was a young girl, but older and even more beautiful with her dark long flowing hair. She introduced Nin to the family while she picked up each baby and kissed it. Nin was tall and nice looking with slightly graying hair and seemed very devoted to Willer Mae, the way he put his arm around her waist while they all stood outside in the front of the house getting acquainted. The house was surrounded by woods, and Charlie had not seen another house for the last mile.

"am so glad ya'll got to come back here to see us," Willer Mae told them." Aw been a saving our money so we can come out to California in maybe four or five years from now and see ya all."

"Well that will give us something to look forward to, sister. Then I won't feel so bad about leaving ya and going back," said Naomer.

"Aw cooked a big pot of chili beans and made corn bread when aw thought ya might be here," Willer Mae went on with her dark eyes dancing, "aw bet ya'lls hungry. Aw made some mashed potatoes for these sweet babies and baked some apples."

The smell of chili, corn bread baking and cinnamon on the baked apples, lingered in the house when they stepped into it. The old walls needed painting badly, and their furnishings looked like hand me downs that had not been taken care of. A large blanket lay over the lumpy sofa concealing the broken springs. There were several other overstuffed chairs in the room with fresh white dollies on the arms and at the head rest. Everything looked clean and smelled fresh.

While they were eating dinner a knock was heard at the front door and Nin went to answer it.

"Aw'll be back in awhile. Ya'll go ahead and eat," he hollered back to the family as he went out the door.

"That's a customer for some moonshine," Willer Mae told them quietly.

"Nin has a stil here?" asked Naomer surprised.

"Well, yeah, didn't Francis and Roy tell ya'll. It's out in the woods some."

'But isn't that illegal?" asked Naomer.

"Well, it is if ya git caught by the revenuers. Most people in these parts knows he's got it. Even the sheriff's come and get five gallons at a time and than puts it in half pints and sells it to the drunks down town on the other side of the tracks. Then the police arrest the same people for being drunk," Willer Mae told her family.

"Why that's down right sinful," Naomer spoke up.

"Aw don't like it either, sister, but Nin can make a whole lot more money with a stil than he can doing roofing work. There's just nobody building homes much now," stated Willer Mae.

"Now sis don't say anything about the stil to Nin," Francis jumped in, "It just causes a rift between him and Willer Mae."

"But sister," Naomer touched Willer Mae's cheek, "You're so beautiful. You could do so much better then this. Aw know he's good looking and tall and aw guess good to you, but what if he goes to the penitentiary?" asked Naomer.

"Aw love him. Aw guess aw just have to take that chance," answered Willer Mae.

Everyone was quite for awhile as they sat around the table finishing their meal. Nin returned and sat at his place not mentioning a word about where he had went. The men continued their talking at one end of the table while the women were at the opposite end. The babies were finishing eating and getting restless.

"I think I'll get the babies bathed and ready for a nap," Naomer said. "Charlie will you help me with the water?"

"There's a pan of hot water on the cook stove," Willer Mae informed her. "Aw'll git ya a big pan to bath them in and we'll put it on the sink top."

The men went into the living room to smoke, and Willer Mae and Francis started clearing the table and stacked the dishes up to be washed after Naomer bathed the babies. After everything was done, they all played cards at the table and talked the rest of the day. The coal oil lamps served as lights, casting shadows on the walls, making the room cozy and content while they enjoyed each other's company.

The next day while the women rocked the babies and were engrossed in a conversation about their childhood, and the men were sitting out on the front porch chewing tobacco and talking, Charlie slipped out the back way towards the outdoor toilet and through the woods to see if he could find the stil. He had no idea what a stil looked like except for information he picked up from the men's conversation. He followed a pathway through the thick woods about a quarter of a mile until it ended. The woods were vibrant with fall colors. He came upon a clearing and instilled the memory of it in his mind as his eyes swept across the hills and hollers. He was amazed at the beauty of it. His thoughts ran back to the beautiful pine and ceder trees in the mountains in California. Where he lived now, in San Joaquin Valley, the land consisted mostly of farm land and vineyards. Not so pretty, but with an abundance of crops that according to his social studies class in school compared to no other place in United States.

He started back along the path into the forest looking around but not seeing any place that might look like a stil was hidden. He noticed one direction was not as thick with brush and trees so he walked that way and stopped when he got a scent of a certain odor. He followed the odor, clearing his way through the brush, and walked upon a large tank which looked to him like it held about two hundred gallons, judging it by the milk cans he had hauled on the route at home. It had a low fire under it which was built in a rock pit. The tank had copper coils leading from it into a closed pot. A girgling noise made it sound creepy as Charlie stared at the monsterous stil for a long time. Wait till I tell the boys back home about this, he though. He walked around it looking it over pretty good before he decided he better go back to the house before he was missed.

Charlie didn't tell anyone he had been gone and no one seemed to miss him. Several people came at different times that day and Nin would take them out back to a locked shed and then they would leave.

The women were still engrossed in their conversation around the table while the babies all slept, and the men were still sitting on the porch talking, where Charlie joined them.

"Well, Charlie," Roy acknowledged him in his slow speech, "Ed was just a telling us that you lived on a ranch where they kept rodeo stock. Tell us about it, son.

Charlie started telling them about being boarded at the ranch that he hated so much. He was glad they wanted to hear about it, as he loved to talk, and to this point of their visit no one had asked him much of anything.

In the kitchen Francis and Willer Mae wanted to hear all about Naomer's and Charlie's lives after they left Alabama.

"Well, I kind of liked San Francisco and Oakland. They are exciting towns. Always something going on there. They're surrounded by the ocean. Oh sisters, ya'll should see the ocean. It's the most beautiful thing aw ever seen. The water goes in and out on the white sandy beaches and rocks making the most heavenly sounds, and the smell is something like ya never smelled before. Like seaweed, and fish and fresh air all mixed together. Big birds called Seagulls fly everywhere, and ya see a lot of Sealions too on the rocks. Oh and the skyscrapers at night when all the lights are on is a sight to behold. Why you wouldn't believe they could make buildings that high. I would of never believed it if I wouldn't of seen it with my own eyes. Oh I didn't tell any of ya that I worked at a show dance place. I was afraid that Momma and Daddy wouldn't approve and worry about me." I didn't have any work experience and that was the only job I could find at the time."

Francis and Willer Mae's mouths dropped open. "It was a nice place though. Only richer folks could afford to come there. We just put on shows that we danced in."

"Did ya date a lot of the guys there?" asked Willer Mae.

"No, well I guess I did date a couple of times. I was asked out a lot, but most of them I wouldn't date." She went on changing the subject. "Poor little Charlie though, he didn't like the big city and kept wanting to move back to Alabama. He missed ya'll so much at first. Then we moved with my boyfriend, Jake, up to the mountains. It was beautiful there too. The Pine Trees and Cedar and Redwoods were so pretty, especially when it snowed. Charlie loved it up there. The towns are small like Guntersville and everyone knows ya.

"Tell us what was Jake like?" asked Francis.

"Oh, he was my friend. I could talk with him about anything. He always understood and was very smart. He was so good to me and Charlie and wanted me to marry him. But I wasn't ready yet to settle down, and I guess the passion just wasn't there with him. Not like it was with Ed anyways. After Momma died I started to drink a lot with the other waitresses where I worked at Murphy's Hotel. Charlie was boarded out and it was a lot easier to come home to an empty house after a few drinks and sleep. I know I neglected Charlie a lot during that time. But it seemed to be something aw had to go through after Momma died."

"Well, it looks like Charlie turned out pretty good." Francis acknowledged. "We all took Momma's death real hard."

In the late afternoon they all said their good bys to Willer Mae and Nin and went with Francis and Roy to R.T.'s home. It too was a little shack in the woods, but closer to Carl and Safronie's home in Birmingham. Naomer hugged her brother and his new wife, Gladyes, as she introduced them to Ed and the children.

"Aw can't reckon you're already fourteen," R.T. said, as he hugged Charlie. "Ya were such a little feller when ya left us. Remember that pet squirrel ya had in your pocket at Francis and Maggie's wedding and it got out? Boy that caused some commotion."

"Yeah, I sure do," answered Charlie, "I sure thought I was gonna be in trouble that time."

"Well, I never heard about that, Charlie," Ed said.

"Aw never did neither," added Glaydes, "Tell us about it."

"You tell them, Uncle R.T., I was too little to remember much about it."

R.T., Francis, and Naomer, all told about the double wedding and the squirrel incident while everyone roared with laughter.

The next day Charlie and his family were on their way to Maggie's home closer to Guntersville. Naomer was drying her eyes from crying over leaving her family. From Maggie's they would head back to California. Lillian and Bill had moved on to Georgia for Bill to take a job there,

Naomer and her family would not be able to go there because of time for Ed to get back to his job.

"I enjoyed visiting with my family so much," she said, "Did ya like them all, Ed.?"

"Sure, I had a real nice time. I really did enjoy just sitting around talking about hunting and fishing and things," answered Ed.

"Well, you've worked so hard over the last several years. Early and late hours and lifting those heavy milk cans," she added. "You too, Charlie, on the milk route and a taking care of all your animals. And helpin with the babies. Just look at these sweet little things sleepin away." Rose was asleep on a blanket on the back seat next to Charlie and Edward was asleep on a pallet on the floor below Rose. Naomer held the baby while he slept.

Maggie had her five children lined up in the living room when Naomer's family entered the door. Louise, the oldest, was holding the baby. Maggie introduced all the children to each other with Naomer's help and told Louise to take them all to the boy's bedroom to play. She put the baby in a cradle in the living room by the grownups.

Charlie followed Louise, who looked to be about nine, to help her take care of the children, and to help serve the sandwiches that Maggie had already made up, along with milk for the kids. The four small children sat around a child's play table.

One of the twin beds, covered with a colorful handmade quilt, served as a seating place for Charlie and Louise. The grownups had sandwiches and coffee around the kitchen table in the modest small home that Maggie's husband, Emery, had recently built for them. He worked hard in the coal mines and made good pay, which enabled them to save up enough to build their home, Maggie explained.

"My, it sure is a lovely home!" exclaimed Naomer.

"We're all just so comfortable here, compared to the little home we all were a livin in," Maggie said. "We just couldn't keep it warm in the winter. It had so many cracks in it that we were just a cutting wood all the time. But aw think this here house will hold the heat pretty good."

"Well, aw should think so woman," Emery sniffled, "Aw built this house to last. Come on, Ed, we'll go outside and aw'll show you some of the work on it.

Naomer looked at her sister as Maggie cleared the table. She had put on some weight, probably from having five children she guessed. Maggie's large round dark eyes danced as they talked, trying to catch up on the years they were apart.

"I feel sorry for Francis and little Willer Mae. Why they live in nothing but shacks," Naomer said, "But don''t you tell them I said that."

"Aw know, sister, but they're happy. Why Roy treats Francis like a queen. And Willer Mae is so in love. Nin must treat her pretty good. She says he does."

"Well, I'm worried about our little sister. How in the world did she ever get mixed up with someone making moonshine?" asked Naomer.

"Now, don't go a frettin about that too much, Sister. There's a lot of men making moonshine back here, and aw ain't never yet seen one go to jail for it. This might be a dry state, but the police officers and the moon shiners got behind the church people and pushed to make it illegal, so's it could be a black market," Maggie went on.

Naomer looked astonished, "Why it kind of defeated the good people's purpose and made it worst. Maybe they should reverse the law. I just want Willer Mae to be happy, and I don't know how she could be too happy with that hanging over her head."

"Well sis, aw don't see her too much. But she always seems to be happy when aw do see her, and goes on about him like he's a knight in shinning armor."

"What about Francis? You say Roy is really good to her?" Naomer ask.

"Oh he lets Francis boss him around like an ole Army Sargeant," answered Maggie. "Roy's quiet. Did ya hear him play the fiddle?"

"Oh yes, he's marvelous on the fiddle. He sure is a little scrawny thing, but he sure can make that fiddle talk."

"Did they tell you he plays with a big band sometimes, and they even played at the Grand ole Opry."

"Yes, Francis was a braggin about that."

"Now what about you, Maggie, are ya happy and content?" Naomer asked somberly.

"Yes Mame. My Emery is so good to me and the kids. We can't afford to do much or go much, but am just content cooking and taking care of my little family."

Naomer laugh, "Now five kids ain't exactly a little family,"

"Well, four ain't neither, Sis, when they're that close together as yours."

"Well, aw think Momma would be mighty pleased with all of us. I surely wish she could see all of the grandchildren." Naomer said, as she gazed out the kitchen window with her thoughts of their mother.

In the children's bedroom Charlie and Louise glanced at each other while they watched the younger children play. Louise was shy and ducked her head when Charlie looked at her.

"Ya must have been born right after my ma and me moved to California," he said to her.

"Aw just turned nine a few weeks ago," she answered. "What's California like?"

Charlie was glad she was finally going to talk to him. "Oh, the same as here. almost. Looks the same. Cept ya have a lot more trees here than where I live now. We use to live in the mountains, and there's a lot of tall pine trees and Manzanita bushes, and deer and mountain lions and bear up there too."

"Ooh, that sounds scary. There's some wild animals here too, but we never see them, cept for deer," Louise said, as she gazed at her image in the mirror attached to an old dresser. A girl with short light brown hair, freckles and hazel eyes gazed back. She twisted her head slightly, proud of her image, until Charlie glanced at her in the mirror and she turned her head embarrassed that she had been admiring herself.

The thoughts were gone as little Edward and Ovader started fighting over a teddy bear. Louise grabbed another teddy bear. "Here little sister, You play with this one and let your cousin have that one."

"Do you have a girlfriend?" Louise asked Charlie suddenly.

"Na, girlfriends are too much trouble. They don't want you to play sports or do anything cept hang around with them. Maybe a couple of years from now I'll have time for a girl friend," answered Charlie, while he looked in the mirror and combed his hair.

The next morning they got an early start toward home. The sun was just rising, and the pink golden light gave promise of a new day ahead.

Naomer wiped her eyes from crying again over leaving her family behind. "Aw may never see them again," she cried.

"Of course you will," answered Ed, "They'll come out and see us, and we'll come back here again, I promise," he assured her.

Charlie wiped his eyes secretly, not wanting his folks to know he had tears in them.

"Mommy cry," Eward said as he rubbed his mother's cheek.

"No, your mommy's okay now. After all I have ya'll to make me happy," she said as she kissed him on the forehead.

Two days later they were driving along the highway in the desert when they drove past a car with the hood up and a man beside it looking bewildered. It was only the end of October, but a cold snap had hit and it was very cold outside the warm car.

"Oh that poor mans a having car trouble and it's so cold out there. Maybe we should stop and help him, Ed," exclaimed Naomer. The car was going the opposite direction so Ed slowed down and turned the car around stopping a short distant behind the other car.

"Charlie you stay here with the kids," Naomer said as she got out of the car with Ed."

"Are you having trouble?" Ed asked the medium size built man that had a long trench coat and hat on.

"Yeah, it just died on me all of a sudden and I can't seem to get it started," he answered, kind of nervously.

"My husband here does a lot of mechanic work, maybe he can fix it," Naomer said, as Ed was already looking under the hood.

"Where ya headed too?" asked Naomer.

"Kansas," the man answered kind of sharply.

"Looks like your water pump belt has broken," Ed said, still looking under the hood.

"So means I need a new one?" he asked.

"Looks that way. We can take ya to the next town if ya can get a ride back here,"

The man didn't say anything. He was silent like he was thinking. Than he reached into his coat and pulled a gun out, pointing it at them.

"You're gonna stay here and I'm going to take your car," he said.

"Oh my God, we have four babies with us," Naomer screamed.

Charlie was watching all this, and had the window cracked so he could bearly hear what they were saying. The man had his back turned toward Charlie. Charlie grabbed a glass pop bottle from the floor board and quietly opened the car door, telling the kids to stay there. Ed noticed what Charlie was doing and kept talking loudly to the man to keep his attention so Charlie could sneak up behind him. Charlie raised the bottle coming down hard with it across the man's head and they all watched as he fell to the ground, out cold. Ed grabbed the gun still in his hand.

"Good work Charlie, Ed said. Let's put him inside his car and we'll hurry to the next town and report him and turn this gun in."

"Oh my Lord, Charlie, you probably saved all out lives," Naomer cried, as they hurried back to their warm car and took off in the direction close to a town.

At the next town seven miles down the highway they learned the man had robbed a bank and shot one of the tellers. They had to give a report to the police and a reporter took their story. They were also told the man was a dangerous mobster from Kansas City.

They were glad to be back on the road and anxious to get home. The rest of the trip was quiet. The children were wore out and slept most of the way. Charlie read funny books and they all listened to Fiber MaGee and Molly, Amos and Andy and other programs on the radio. This time of togetherness Charlie would always remember. Ed even seemed closer to him, Charlie thought. Like he really enjoyed his company.

When they pulled into their driveway in Lockeford, Charlie heaved a sigh of relief. They were home. There was Venture waiting at the gate to greet them. Tony raised his head up in the pasture and all the other animals seem to turn toward them and look.

Charlie's thoughts raced over the last several weeks. Wait till I tell everyone about Alabama, and the stil, and the bank robber he thought. He would always remember his family in Alabama, his birth family, but there wasn't another place in the world that he would rather be than right here at home. He would travel again someday, and have great adventures when he grew up. There would still be sad times and good times. Perhaps he would go over seas to fight in a war; perhaps a career to pursue; and perhaps he would have a wife and children someday. There was so much to look forward to. But in the mean time he would continue dreaming those silver lined dreams right here at home.

THE END